Crumbs from the Master's Table

Book one of Servants by Blood Vampire

Series

By K.A. Monaco

DEDICATION

To God: Thanks for the creativity.
To my husband: for inspiration, believing in me, unconditional love and long
suffering while enduring the endless revisions.
And to my family: for those who supported me, thank you.

Table of Content:

Chapter 1

1928

Rebecca's eyes flittered open. The light from the passing street light lit the interior of the vehicle. The car tilted to round a corner. She felt something move that propped up her head. With a flash of the light, she saw an older man's face, bearded with pale skin. He wore a wool outer jacket with a fur lapel, a wealthy man's attire.

The interior of the car had been upholstered lavishly. A window in the car's roof let in the street light while wallpaper adorned around it. She heard the clinking of glass as the car traversed bumps. Not her first time in a car, but never one this fancy and with a ride so smooth.

Another man sat in the shadows across from her that she only noticed when he moved. The men muttered low, and the meaning of the words escaped her at times as she lapsed into intermittent unconsciousness. The car smelled of cologne. She felt strangely tired, yet warm and comfortable. A type of euphoria lingered in her limbs, like a sedative.

A flash of lightning rippled across the sky revealing the tall buildings from the darkness. A crack of thunder followed. And she knew this was her home, New York City. The windshield wipers squeaked and thumped in rhythm across the glass as the drizzle gently fell.

"Lord Devlin," the man above her said. "I beseech you to change your mind. We need to find a hospital."

"We don't have time," the man in the shadows said with a strong English accent. "At the rate she's losing blood she won't make it. We'd have to travel further into the city. There they will evaluate her and a surgeon will need to be called. I estimate she's lost a half a pint already. By the time the surgeon arrives, she will have lost another two."

"That's about right," the older man said. "How do you know that?"

"I just do."

"But I'm only a general practitioner."

"But they made you operate at least in practice before they licensed you, didn't they?"

"Well, yes," the older man admitted.

"All you can do is your best. You're the only chance she has."

The auto turned a corner, transversed a gutter bouncing all the passengers gently. From Rebecca's vantage point, they entered an alley behind a large house. One more turn and the streetlights were no more.

A five-story home towered in the rear window for an instant as the car entered a garage beneath it. Rebecca felt the car stop. The driver departed first, opening the driver-side rear door, which permitted an influx of cool, damp air. The man supporting Rebecca's head helped the other man as they both lifted her. Rebecca recognized Lord Devlin as he leaned forward to grab her legs. The older man's hands supported her under her arms.

"Oh, what happened? Why are you carrying me?" Rebecca asked. She lifted her hand from her chest to see blood on her fingertips. She panicked as her voice turned shrill. "I'm bleeding? I'm bleeding!"

"You've been shot," Devlin said. "Stay calm."

"How did it happen?" Rebecca asked. The events of the evening were sketchy.

"You stepped between me and the man with the gun."

"Let me get her, Lord Devlin," the older man at her head said.

"No, I've got her, Doctor Wells," Lord Devlin said as he stood from exiting the car. Devlin easily slipped his arm beneath her knees then around her back. She wrapped her arm around his neck and shoulder. "She's just a little thing, not heavy at all."

Dr. Wells adjusted Rebecca's overcoat that wrapped around her. Then, another man appeared by the house, a silhouette at the top of the stairs. When he passed before the headlights, Rebecca recognized a butler's uniform on the small-statured man.

"Up the stairs, doctor," Lord Devlin said.

What's going on? Who are these people? Where am I?

The doctor passed the butler and headed for the house. A

surreal sensation increased as Rebecca began to feel pain. She moaned as Devlin carried her. The chauffeur shut the door to the back passenger area of the vehicle. Then another figure stood in the doorway, a tall woman in a traditional dark floor-length skirt. Not the flapper fashion of the day.

"What about the other one, Lord Devlin?" the driver asked.

"Bring him in as well, Carmichael," Lord Devlin said to the chauffeur. He jostled Rebecca and she tensed in pain. "Sorry, love. To the basement. That's where we're all headed. Roberts, I'm glad you're still up."

Devlin Englewood, a good dancer and such a pleasant English accent. I could listen to that all night.

Struck by dizziness, everyone's movements and voices revolved around her like a kaleidoscope. She struggled to discern any of it. The pain in her abdomen worsened. Roberts, the butler, approached.

"What happened?" Roberts asked.

"Are you hurt, my Lord?" the tall woman asked concerned, crooking her neck to see Rebecca. An older woman with fluffy black hair tied up in an old-fashioned bun. Her face lined with modest wrinkles about her eyes. Rebecca detected kindness or pity in her hazel eyes.

"No, Eva," Devlin replied to the woman, then addressed the butler again. "This woman stepped between me and a bullet."

"Oh," Roberts said. "Why didn't you take her to a hospital? Why have you brought her here? We're not equipped for this sort of thing, unless helping her was not your intent?"

"She stepped between me and a bullet," Devlin snarled. "I'm not dumping her on the doorstep of strangers, and you know my attitude about women. Now help Carmichael with the other passenger."

"I'll fetch some bandages and water," Eva said, disappearing.

Like in a dream, Rebecca saw the butler as he joined the chauffeur at the car's rear. Carmichael opened the trunk, and both reached in to drag out the unconscious man she knew as Tony Too Tall, her boyfriend.

Lord Devlin headed into the house. She lost sight of the car as Devlin mounted the four steps and angled her through the door frame with precarious precision. Once inside, Rebecca noticed the grand decor of the house; plush carpets, pristine wallpaper all in matching tones, and high ceilings with crown moldings.

"This isn't a hospital." Rebecca closed her eyes and moaned again. "It's a mansion."

"Just a little farther," Devlin said.

Devlin joined the doctor as they rushed down another set of stairs. Rebecca lost consciousness for a little but woke when she felt the release of the arms beneath her. A cold seeped through her overcoat from the smooth table. Curiosity caused her to observe her surroundings. Mysterious dark shadows of odd furnishings along the outer walls caught her eye and gave off an eeriness to the large room. Nearby were strange tables and objects, old relics with spotlights over them.

by K.A. Monaco

This place looks more like the Spanish Inquisition dungeon from the wax museum.

"Where am I?" Rebecca asked.

"You're in my home," Devlin replied. Blood dotted his face, clothes, and hands. He brushed his nose, smearing more blood on his face. "Don't move. Stay still, little one."

"Little one?" Rebecca laughed, but it hurt. "Because I'm little in size. You're very handsome."

"She's intoxicated," Dr. Wells muttered.

"No, it's something else. But it's wearing off quickly." Devlin moved toward her upper body, pulling a stool on squeaky wheels under him to sit closer. "Why did you do this, little one? Why did you try to protect me?"

"Tony accused you wrongly," Rebecca said. "But now—I wished he was right. Ohhhh, I don't feel well."

"You're a very brave young woman," Devlin said. "But now you must be much braver."

Rebecca tried to sit up, but the pain shot through her like the lightning she witnessed outside. Devlin restrained her. Eva, the woman from the garage, towered over her. Her thin, tall stature, leaned over Rebecca's mid-section.

She caught a glimpse of herself, Lord Devlin, and Eva in a long mirror. They had laid her on a white porcelain pedestal table the likes of which she had never seen before. Devlin's face flashed grim, nervously glanced at Eva, and Rebecca's hopes diminished.

I don't want to die. I'm too young.

"Am I dying?" Rebecca faced Devlin. "Please help me."

"Calm, stay calm," Devlin said in a velvety smooth tone. "You'll only make it worse if you struggle."

"I must remove the bullet, but I'll need some help," Dr. Wells said.

"Eva." Devlin pointed a bloody hand at the doctor. Eva nodded and moved in position to help while Devlin watched the door nervously from Rebecca's side.

"But I don't have any anesthesia?" Dr. Wells said, laying open her coat. "Oh, this is a mess. I only heard before how a nine-millimeter bullet could make such a mess at close range. They were right."

Devlin turned his head, pressing his nose and mouth against his upper arm. He looked distressed. Rebecca noticed a hungry look in his eyes, but only for a moment.

"She's lost so much blood," Dr. Wells muttered.

"Tell me what I can do, doctor," Eva said.

"I'll sedate her, just tell me when," Devlin said. "But hurry up."

"Does the sight of blood bother you, Lord Devlin?" The doctor ripped at her dress, jerking her midsection to expose the bullet wound. Rebecca let out a cry.

"Be gentle," Devlin snapped, cringing more.

"Perhaps another should take your place. You'd never make a doctor," Dr. Wells said. "Madam, look in my bag for scissors."

"Never wanted to be one," Devlin replied focusing back on

Rebecca. "Young woman, stay with me. What is your name?"

"Rebecca Bellows," Rebecca said closing her eyes in fear.

She could hear Eva digging in the black bag. A pair of scissors caught the light as Eva handed them to the doctor. He cut the dress over her pelvis and fileted it open. Rebecca felt the cool air hit parts of her that decency said shouldn't be exposed and impulsively moved to cover it. Devlin grabbed her hands and held them. She tried to pull free, but the effort caused sharp pains in her midsection. She gasped.

"You can't touch. The doctor must do his work," Devlin said. She could feel his face next to hers as his cold hands restrained her. She nodded and he released his hold. But she quickly grabbed them and squeezed as the pain worsened with the doctor's examination. She clenched her teeth and let out a whimper.

"That's right," Devlin whispered. "Squeeze my hands. I'm here to help you."

Rebecca looked over at some commotion at the door. Roberts and Carmichael, dumped the body of Tony in a heap on the floor. Blood trickled down his face and neck into his collar now crimson-stained. They discarded him rather disrespectfully beside a large stone wall. Carmichael stood at her feet, observing.

Tony. You shot me? I thought you loved me. No, you only used me.

Carmichael leaned over the open wound on Eva's side when she pushed him back.

"I just wanted to see," Carmichael said. "I can smell her ...

blood." His eyes rolled back in his head.

"*No*, Carmichael," Devlin snapped. "*No*."

"He's a ripe one," Carmichael motioned to Tony. "But she's so small."

"Know your place, Carmichael," Eva growled.

Tony moaned.

"He's awakening," Devlin said. "Put him on the rack. I'll deal with him later."

Carmichael and Roberts grabbed Tony again. They hoisted him onto one of the devices in the room. Roberts pulled Tony's arms to his side while attaching metal cuffs linked to heavy chains. Rebecca watched as Roberts turned a wheel on the side of the device, and the chain went taut lifting Tony's arms over his head. Tony sluggishly shifted his weight while waking. Carmichael hurried, placing similar cuffs with chains on his ankles. When the wheel became hard to turn, Carmichael took over, making it snug. Roberts rubbed Tony's neck until it was pink and the vein's surfaced under the skin.

"What are you doin' to me?" Tony shrieked and fought his restraints. "I have friends in high places. You're askin' for trouble."

Then Robert's shoved a rag in Tony's mouth. "Your friends can't help you now."

"What will you do to him?" Rebecca asked Devlin hovered over her.

"He's a violent man, love," Devlin sneered, with a quick glare back at Tony. She felt his hand gently caress the side of her face. It calmed her. Everything about this man made her feel safe.

"He hit you, then shot you, and he doesn't deserve you," Devlin continued. "No man should beat a woman. It only shows what a weak-minded, low life he is."

"Lord Devlin, I'm ready," Dr. Wells said.

"You need to take a little nap, sweet girl," Devlin said. "Listen to my voice."

He leaned over her, tilting her chin to the left. She felt a pinch just below her ear on her neck. The pain vanished, and she couldn't fight her eyes from closing.

"Sleep now," Devlin whispered.

All went black.

Chapter 2

Recovery

Rebecca awoke. Devlin hovered over her while she lay weak and exhausted in a large bed. The room adorned lavishly, she felt warm beneath the generous blankets. But on her forehead, the cool sensation of a wet washcloth brought her more out of her grogginess. Devlin's weight shifted the mattress as he dipped the cloth in the water basin, rung the water out and replaced it over her brow.

"I'm sorry," Rebecca said. "I'm not well enough for a game of chess today."

Devlin smiled and patted her hand. "That's fine. I understand."

Over his shoulder, she recognized Roberts and Dr. Wells.

"Are you hungry?" Devlin asked.

She shook her head no. Her fever drained her of every desire except sleep.

"Now how will you get better if you don't eat?" Devlin patronized, his eyes full of compassion. His smile gave her hope.

Devlin reached for a cup and brought it close. She felt hands on her other side help her sit up as he tipped the cup for her to sip.

Lukewarm water wet her dry, cracked lips, moistened her cotton mouth, and soothed her parched throat. Rebecca collapsed back on the pillow.

"I don't understand," Rebecca muttered. "I thought I was getting better."

"We all are still hopeful. Healing takes time." Devlin paused. "Rebecca, I'm leaving for a spell but will return before you know it."

"No, no," Rebecca muttered. She could barely lift her hand to reach out to him. He took her hand in his cold clasp, kissed her fingers, and met her fearful gaze. "Why?"

"I have businesses in Europe that need my attention. I travel much."

"And I've kept you from what you need to do, I'm sorry."

"I'm not. But, in my absence, everyone here will take good care of you, I promise." Devlin leaned over her. "I'll suckle you just before I leave. Rest and I'll be back soon."

Rebecca nodded, closed her eyes, and felt his cold lips against her cheek. Then the bed shifted, and she knew Devlin had stood. The washcloth moved, and she opened her eyes to see Eva on her other side adjusting it. Eva sympathetically smiled down at her. Rebecca closed her eyes again waiting for sleep again.

"Eva, please assist Lord Devlin with his packing," Roberts instructed.

"Yes, sir," Eva replied. She bowed slightly and scooted off the bed.

The men watched quietly until Eva left.

"We need to get her out of this house and to a hospital," Dr. Wells said. "I can't help her any more here."

The doctor walked closer, picked up her wrist and felt her pulse.

"The fever is too high," Dr. Wells continued. "And her heart rate, for being sedentary, is too rapid. I'd like my colleagues to assess her. I'm quite pleased with how the bullet wound healed so quickly in the last month. But now the fever worries me. It's a sign of infection, but where is the source?"

"I want her gone as much as you want to get her to a hospital," said Roberts. "Wait till the master has left. Bring an ambulance around, and you can have her."

"But Lord Devlin forbids her removal, you heard him deny my many attempts."

"My master will be gone for nearly a month with another sea voyage to Europe. When he returns, I'll simply tell him she died. Can I count on you for a death certificate?"

"That goes against my Hippocratic Oath," Wells replied. "Why do you hate her?"

"People like her are a drain on the staff and Lord Devlin's purse strings," Roberts snarled. "He's too soft-hearted and feels guilty for what his actions did to her. But she's riffraff and deserves what she gets. He shouldn't feel obligated to care for society's train wrecks. She's no better than the Jews and the poor."

"I don't share your sentiments," Wells replied. "I'm trying to save her life. You're beginning to sound like that fascist from

Germany."

The doctor paused in thought. Too tired to continue watching them, she closed her eyes again, but listened.

"Will you do it?" Roberts asked.

"Do what?"

"Remove her by an ambulance?"

"*No*," Wells replied. "After seeing what Lord Devlin did to the man that shot her. I feel both privileged and horrified in knowing his identity. But I won't go against his wishes for all his money."

"Very well, then I will take matters into my own hands," Robert said and walked away.

Rebecca heard their feet softly brushing the carpet and knew they had left. Alone, she passed out again.

***

Rebecca stirred to the sound of coughing, groans, and hard sole shoes shuffling against a flat surface. By the sounds, she concluded she no longer resided in the manor, as all the floors there were carpeted. The noises were strange, the voices too low to decern, and the essence of sanitizer accosted her olfactory senses. The mix of alcohol and ammonia, each having its pre-eminence depending on which way the air moved.

Rebecca struggled to open her eyes. The harsh overhead lighting made the sterile white curtains glow which separated the beds. A community room in a hospital. Remembering the men's ward when her father returned from war, she recognized this as the women's by the higher-pitched voices.

Looking down at her feet, a clipboard swayed on the outer side of the bed rail, and a man in a white coat stood facing her. The man was not Dr. Wells, the doctor Lord Devlin retained for her care.

"You're awake?" the man in the white coat asked.

Rebecca nodded.

"I'm Doctor Smyth," he said as he detached the clipboard, and moved to her side pulling up a chair. "Your fever broke last night, finally."

She nodded again.

"It's amazing you're alive," Dr. Smyth said. "Tossed out of a moving car, a skull fracture and two broken legs resulted in high fevers over a two-month coma. None of us thought you'd pull through, Miss."

Rebecca nodded again and felt faint. His words only slightly making sense.

I was tossed from a car?

"Are you in any pain?" Smyth asked.

She shook her head no.

"I need you to speak."

Rebecca could tell by his accent he was from New England, maybe Boston.

"No pain." Her voice cracked as her mouth and throat felt like a desert.

"Good." he smiled with crooked teeth as he wrote on the clipboard. "Do you know your name?"

"Rebecca."

"And your last name?" he asked. She shook her head again. "It's not uncommon. Give it a day and you may remember."

"Why am I here? And where am I?"

"You're in a hospital, recovering."

"Yes, but which one?"

"St. Mary's in Newark, New Jersey," he said. Rebecca nodded, not that St. Mary's, Peter, or Paul would have been more relevant. "Do you know the date?"

"No." She hesitated. "Maybe late October?"

"No," Smyth said, writing again. "Do you know the year?"

"1928?"

"Close, 1929, and it's early March, to be exact. You arrived here in January. Do you remember anything that happened to you?"

"I was shot."

"Well, yes, but that was an older wound," the doctor began. "A full examination revealed the projectile penetrated your body, probably causing significant damage to your reproductive organs necessitated their removal. The attending physician must have had to make a critical decision to preserve your life. Regrettably, it was necessary to perform a hysterectomy and oophorectomy."

"I don't know what that means," she said.

"I am truly sorry, but it means you're unable to bear children. Do you remember any of this?"

Rebecca nodded. "Doctor Wells was the physician." She tried to sit up, but the doctor restrained her.

"Don't try to rise yet. So, the physician who did the surgery was a Doctor Wells?"

Rebecca nodded again.

"I'll look into that. Do you remember which hospital?"

"Not in a hospital, a private home," she replied.

"I see, how unusual."

"Why can't I get out of bed?" she asked. "Did you say I had broken bones. How?"

"You arrived by ambulance after you were tossed out of a moving automobile. Eyewitnesses said it was a red Duesenberg. Would you happen to know who it was?"

Rebecca shook her head, not recognizing the name of the automobile.

Is my name Rebecca? Devlin? It was he who helped me, and in his home. The surgery rendered me unable to have children? I can't have children.

The doctor droned on as she fixated on that one fact.

"Miss, did you hear me?" Smyth asked.

"No," Rebecca said, dizzy.

"I asked you if you had any family we can call; a mother and father, or a husband?"

Rebecca shrugged remembering faces and first names but much of it was a fog. She told him a street name that she thought they lived on but nothing concrete. Smyth wrote it down.

"Very good," Smyth said. "I'm impressed you know as much as you do. My first concern was the fractured skull, but you seem to have healed from that. Though you might have some episodic memory loss. Some patients with marked pyrexia psychotic break or have mild cognitive impairment from the fevers alone. I'll see if I can contact your family and this Doctor Wells." The doctor rose and set the chair back. "You'll be with us for a little while yet. Bed-bound for over two months with multiple broken bones, you will have difficulty walking, and we should conduct some psychometric tests to assess any possible brain damage from the coma. And until we can find out who you are, you will be our Jane Doe. I'll be back soon."

"I'm hungry," Rebecca said.

"That's a good sign," the doctor replied. "The nurse will be around with some porridge to start you off."

***

The absence of engagement with anyone else brought the echoes of the doctor's words ringing in her mind. She had never faced a day before that seemed so bleak. Hours drifted by, the hands on the clock moved, but Rebecca had no concept of it passing. Before, she hated to waste time, always on the move, heading somewhere to do something. Now she felt stalled and confused.

Who would want me? No man would marry me now.

Rebecca didn't sleep. A day and a night passed, and she wept. She cried until the others in her ward complained and tossed pillows at her to shut up. After three days, her crying stopped, replaced by a longing that ached in her bosom. Though she had never been pregnant, she mourned as if she had.

"I'm sorry, Miss." The doctor returned after three days. "There is no one at the residence you specified. And the Doctor Wells you mentioned, was killed the same week you arrived, mugged and shot in New York City."

"What will happen to me?" Rebecca asked.

"We'll wait to see if more of your memory returns. In the meantime, I'll order some physical therapy."

"When can I leave?"

"Oh, not for a while," Smyth said. "It'll take time for you to get back on your feet after two broken legs."

Rebecca felt lost. Other patients had been released, and new ones arrived, yet she remained, neglected. In the busy ward, few were capable to help her out of bed. Her bones had healed but had left her stiff.

Chapter 3

Lost & Found

Two days later, in the pre-dawn, a frustrated Rebecca tossed the blankets back and sat up. The nurse on duty snored at her desk with her head propped on her hand. Rebecca placed her bare feet on the cold tile floor. The cold had always adversely affected her, but it didn't bother her now. She remembered the doctor told her she would need help walking, but when she rose her muscles obeyed. Step after step, she moved toward the exit door.

"March," Rebecca whispered as she opened the door and looked back. The nurse mumbled but remained asleep. "March 1929."

Once in the hall, Rebecca looked both ways, but there was no one to greet, stop, or even question her. On a rolling table rested a box that read; Lost and Found. She rummaged through it until she found two different boots, both too large, an overcoat, and an old house dress, also gigantic. She slipped them on then trudged down the hall, sliding the boots along with her feet.

Golden letters on the glass door she couldn't read backward stood before her. The desk of women to her right buzzed with activity, but none of them paid her any mind. She pressed on, through the hall, down the stairs, and out a set of heavy, wooden doors. The fact that she could move didn't seem odd to her, yet the same echo chimed in her head: *can't have children.*

The moon case its rays overhead as the morning began. A cool breeze hit her bare ankles and sobered her mind. The boots clomped against the sidewalk sounding louder than she thought they should. She stopped to listen and even the footsteps of others across the street seemed noisier than before. She didn't know what direction to head in, but by noon she crossed the bridge to New York City.

Rebecca walked for hours passing cars and houses, tripped over curbs, and bumped into people as the streets grew congested. But she kept walking. She circled her parent's apartment building three times before she recognized it. The landlord walked out as Rebecca looked up at the windows.

"Excuse me." Rebecca tugged on the old man's coat. "The family on the third floor, are they home?"

"Them?" the man questioned, gruffly. "The old man shot his brains out in the bathroom after his oldest daughter ran off with some lowlife. It was a fucking mess. The wife had to sell the boys into indentured servitude. She took the girls to Wisconsin or Wyoming, or one of those states that began with W, I can't remember. Who are you, friend of the daughter?"

"I'm the daughter," Rebecca said weakly. "Don't you recognize me?"

"You're not Rebecca Bellows," the landlord said.

Am I the oldest daughter? Rebecca? But the doctor at the

hospital called me Jane Doe. That's right, my last name was Bellows.

"She was a dish," the landlord reminisced with lust in his voice. "A real looker. Always dressed like she was gonna be someone, like one of those dames in the magazines. With long brunette hair, the prettiest light blue eyes I ever saw, full pouty lips, and a figure that…" the landlord gave her the once-over glance. "… well, you ain't her."

Rebecca spied an upturned trashcan lid filled with rainwater. Looking down into it, she didn't recognize her own reflection. Her complexion was as pale as the face of a porcelain doll, and her sunken features so shallow that she appeared emaciated. Short, whitish-blond hair replaced her long brunette locks, and her eyes had changed to a deep, dark blue. As she touched her face, she saw herself for the first time, her hands bony and withered with broken, unpainted nails. She was hideous. She couldn't believe her eyes until the landlord poked his head near hers in the reflection, which startled her.

"I have to go," Rebecca said.

"Lunatics," the landlord muttered as he swept the sidewalk. "I should call the police on you."

Rebecca quickly walked away. The last thing she needed was to be locked in another institution. But nothing looked familiar, especially the face that stared back at her in every plate glass window. But apparently her feet weren't done walking. The sun set around her, and she found herself in Central Park. Under a bush, she curled up in the overcoat to keep warm and fell asleep. What she had weren't dreams but more like recounting of life, a voice from the fog repeating her bleak future without children and Robert's voice saying how she was a drain on society.

When dawn came, a policeman rousted her from under the bush as he did all the other vagabonds who took refuge there. She followed some of the people to a soup kitchen, where helpers handed her a bowl of greasy, thin broth. She drank it, but it tasted like nothing.

She reentered the park and emerged on the other side by noon. Before her stood a tall yellow house, as long as a city block and five stories tall. She stared up at it when the front door opened, and a familiar-looking woman with black hair tied up in a bun stepped out with her broom. Rebecca didn't recognize Eva at first and resumed her staring at the house as the woman progressed with her sweeping to the bottom step.

"Shoo now, getaway. We help no vagrants here," the woman said.

"Is this the home of Lord Devlin?" Rebecca whispered.

"Yes, it is," the woman replied, then gasped. "Miss Rebecca?"

Rebecca nodded and couldn't hold back the tears. Eva was the first person to recognize her. Rebecca collapsed beside the wrought-iron fence, clinging to the bars. Eva tossed open the gate while screaming in a shrill tone for help. Once on the other side, Eva pulled Rebecca from the cement and held her lean, frail body in her arms. Soon two men charged down the stairs and out to the front gate.

"Madam Eva," Carmichael said. "What's wrong? Who's that?"

"It's Rebecca," Eva replied. "Rebecca, the one the master searched for."

"My name is Rebecca," Rebecca muttered. "I don't remember …"

"No, it can't be. This woman is of average height. Rebecca was a petite…." Carmichael looked closely at her face. "My God, you're right. How could this happen?"

After a day of walking and a night exposed to the elements of March, Rebecca's body relented to her exhaustion. The two men supported her as Eva held the gate as they carried her through, one under each arm.

"Remember, we had to cut her hair because of the fevers, but it's turned white," Eva replied to them then turned to Rebecca. "Roberts said you died but the master didn't believe him. He looked for you for months. Where have you been? He'll be so relieved to know you're alive."

"Please, don't tell Devlin I'm alive, at least not yet," Rebecca said with more tears. "I don't want him to see me, not like this."

"Take her inside, quickly," Eva said.

"No," Rebecca jerked, but couldn't resist in her weakened condition. "Roberts tossed me from a moving car. He'll do it again or worse. He'll try to kill me. I shouldn't have come here."

"Roberts is gone," Eva said. "He disappeared shortly after Lord Devlin returned."

"He's gone?" Rebecca asked, hopeful.

"He's more than gone," Carmichael chuckled under his breath, but sobered and fell silent with an evil-glare from Eva.

"Let's just say Roberts can't hurt you now," Eva scolded.

"Now, come. Before you make a scene."

"I don't want to be a burden," Rebecca said.

"Lord Devlin appointed me the head of the house; don't worry about that."

Rebecca nodded, and the men helped her up the stairs and into the house.

Chapter 4

1945

Sixteen years passed, and the world turned upside down. The Great Depression and WWII rocked even the Englewood Manor on two continents. The draft didn't affect the household members, but food and fuel supplies became scarce. And for the manor to maintain in such hard times, many of the servants went without pay.

Rebecca was alone in the kitchen with Eva as Eva flipped through the paper at the long oak table. It was just after breakfast, and the kitchen staff were on a break. Late in May, the many showers had darkened the sky for days, and the staff relished the momentary lull in the weather. Even Rebecca soaked in the sun at the sink's window while washing dishes.

"Now that the war in Europe is over," Eva said. "Maybe sugar, coffee, and fuel won't be so expensive. And we can return to eating steaks instead of ground beef and pull the car out of mothballs."

Rebecca acknowledged her with a simple affirmative.

"You're exceptionally quiet since you wandered off last month," Eva said. "Don't ever do that again. You had us all worried."

Rebecca nodded with downcast eyes at the dishes, her back still to the madam. She could hear the paper's rustling behind her.

"Madam Eva?" Rebecca quietly asked.

"Either Madam or Eva," Eva snipped. "It's unnecessary for both, especially when we're alone."

"Yes, ma'am." Rebecca sighed. "I forgot."

Eva waited a moment. "Well? You were going to ask me something."

Rebecca turned and rested her wet hands on the sink edge. Her facial features were still sunken in, and body terribly thin. Her shoulder length hair had no luster and looked whiter in the kitchen lights. She wiped tears away from swollen eyes and a red nose with her sleeve.

"Why have I not aged?" Rebecca asked. Before Eva could reply, Rebecca continued. "I wandered off because I saw my brother's name among the wounded in the paper. It said that he had come to the Bethesda Hospital. I saw him and my mother. I should be in my thirties. My baby brother was a grown man, and my mother had wrinkles and gray hair. I haven't changed since I arrived."

"That's not true," Eva replied. "Your energy returned, and you're not as skinny as you once were. The venom slows our aging."

"But I haven't had venom since Roberts took me away. While all of you have had it more recently."

"That's till the war took the master away," Eva replied. "The master gave you an abundance of venom to keep you alive that you probably won't need suckling for decades. Don't worry; the master will return before you run out." Eva paused. "You said you saw your family; how was your brother?"

"He died." Rebecca's voice revealed her sorrow as she turned back to the sink. "That's why I was gone so long. I remained for the funeral. I even shook my mother's hand, and she never recognized me."

Rebecca heard the chair scratch the wooden floor abruptly. Eva rose and stood over her by the sink. She could feel Eva's displeasure.

"And if she had, what would you have said to her?" Eva demanded. "How would you have explained your absence? Or how your appearance change? You can't reconnect with your past when you're involved here. The secrets we protect aren't just about us but for the master. We are the guardians of these secrets, and no one must know what happens here."

"I understand," Rebecca whispered. Eva moved back to the table. "I wouldn't do anything to jeopardize the master. I just wanted to see them. And when he didn't make it—to pay my respects. Now that I have, I have no other reason to leave."

"Good," Eva said. "Now, drink your juice. Doctor's orders."

"Tastes worse than normal this morning," Rebecca said. "Taste like it turned."

"Strange, I just opened the can."

"Why tomato juice? Everyone else can have orange or grape."

34

"The doctor said tomato."

"I don't remember him saying only tomato."

"I remember distinctly. Perhaps you need to eat *more* tomatoes. We have spaghetti night once a week. How about you eat the leftovers to get more into your diet."

"If you think so." Rebecca stared out the window.

"Do you like mixed drinks?" Eva asked, sounding less harsh. "I make a mean Bloody Mary. Once we resume our socials on Saturday night again, I'll make you one."

"What about the 'Crumbs'," Rebecca asked. "Everyone misses that. What happens at the ceremony?"

"That is for the senior staff," Eva said.

"But Carmichael goes. And he and I arrived here about the same time. Only a few months apart."

"He's an exception due to his position," Eva replied spitefully. "But don't worry, when you're no longer wandering off, invading the library, or disobeying the rules, you might be invited. Merit and seniority are the only way to gain access. Improve and we will see."

"The sign in the library says we have permission."

"It says prohibited."

"You need to find a dictionary and look up how prohibited is spelled. I have every right to read books from there."

"I'll take it up with the master when he returns," Eva snipped.

"Has he written lately?" Rebecca asked. "Could he have be killed?"

"Not him, but yes." Eva pulled a letter from her smock. "It came while you were away. But this letter was addressed to me only and not the household."

"Oh." Rebecca's voice revealed her disappointment.

"Go ahead and read it," Eva dropped it on the table. "Maybe it'll end your *sulking*."

Rebecca wiped off her hands, sat at the table, and unfolded the letter carefully, as if it were an old parchment about to crumble to pieces.

Dear Eva,

Do not share this with the household. I wish them well, but I cannot share with them as I do with you. I have no one to write but you. You're in my thoughts as well.

This war has been harder than those in the past. It seems the new way to wage war has no honor in it. The brutality is even hard for me to stomach at times. It is not just the soldier that feel fear. But you feel it for us. I see it in the faces of the young men. They are not evil, yet they will die for "the cause" by those who may never be held responsible. They say this is the war to end all wars, but there will be war as long as men have greed or lust for power in their hearts.

War has a way of distracting from one's pain and loneliness. Surrounded by greater pain makes my own pale in comparison. When this is over, I know I'll move on from that which almost destroyed me. Yet I still miss her and see her face on those rare occasions that I dream.

Crumbs from the Master's Table

I regret to say the German bombers all but destroyed the Englewood estate in England. Those at the manor escaped without casualty. My servants there recovered what they could of those things that helped me remember my mother and childhood. But compared to so many, my losses are minute.

I know Viktor is behind the scenes in Russia, Phillip is working in the Underground in Paris, and Miguel is pushing troops into Italy. But Hans has disappeared. He has chosen not to fight for either side. I can't blame him. But if he shows up, please do not show prejudice. He is still my family.

I am in Germany now. With the American forces alongside my garrison, we are making much headway. I expect treaties will be signed or this evil rescheme will surrender soon. I know the questions you are asking. Have I seen action? The answer is yes. And I've been wounded several times. (Rebecca gasped; her body became rigid, and her fingers curved over her mouth, but she continued reading.)

But as you know, my wounds aren't life-threatening. I hope no one has presented themselves to announce my untimely demise. But if they have, I'm sorry for the grief and sorrow they caused. I am well in my body.

I have declined many nominations for awards. If they truly knew why I scouted at night and killed without reservation, they would not be so honoring of my skills as a hunter. But war is like that. The bad become heroes and the good die.

It is a relief that the staff is all safe in the States and that none have had to join the fight. I look forward to seeing you and hope your hardships are not too much to bear. I have full faith that you are managing well in my absence.

One good thing this war has produced is the abundance of flying machines. We jumped from a plane into Germany, which both amazed and scared me. But in the dead of night, we fell, deployed our parachutes (which I will explain upon my return), and I could see the great mountains afar off. Air travel will be the next great thing. If I ever sail again, it will be for recreation. Compared to flight, even the train feels laborious.

I must go—they are calling for the mail. I wish you well and promise to return. Do not fear though I know you shall.

Deepest Regards,

Lord Devlin.

Rebecca folded up the paper and slid it back to Eva.

"Thank you," Rebecca mumbled.

I will always love Devlin from the shadows, but looking like this, he must never know I lived. How could he have loved me? He never knew me.

The rest of the kitchen staff returned and took positions at their workstations while Rebecca returned to the dishes. Their chatter was low but cheerful.

"Once the band on travel is lifted," Eva said. "Lord Devlin said he'll be sending us a new butler, Timothy. I always liked that name. I only hope he's better than Roberts."

"What happened to Roberts?" Rebecca asked.

"He died." Eva abruptly pulled the paper before her.

"So did Dr. Wells."

"He did?"

"Right after Roberts took me away. Do you think Roberts killed Dr. Wells?"

"Why would Roberts do that?"

"So the master couldn't find me. I heard them arguing. Dr. Wells refused to put me in a hospital after the master left, and Roberts said he would take it upon himself. Dr. Wells would have told the master what Roberts did."

"Fevers can cause hallucinations," Gretta said.

"It wasn't a hallucination," Rebecca muttered.

"Water under the bridge now." Eva refocused on the paper.

"And what happened to Tony?" Rebecca asked. "I know he died, but how?"

"Ask the master when he returns," Eva replied.

"I can't, not looking like this. I don't want him to see me like this."

"Hopefully, more tomatoes will help." Eva sighed.

"Perhaps." Rebecca returned to her quiet state.

Rebecca could tell Eva's patience was exhausted with her questions. Eva resumed looking at the paper. The staff's conversation became low background noise to Rebecca's loneliness and sorrow.

Chapter 5

2014

Many, many years later, Rebecca walked into the kitchen at the Englewood manor. Her looks improved. Her hallowed appearance was replaced with a radiant complexion and supple skin. But the fevers permanently altered her eyes and hair color. Gone were the sky-blue color eyes and long flowing brown locks. Her fatigue and weakness were also gone. And though she was well enough to leave, she stayed for no better place to go.

"Drink your juice, Becca," Eva said. "The master will be arriving soon."

Eva's short, gray hair teased curly, and her facial flesh sagged, showing her age. An unattractive black and white uniform fell over her bony body, giving her a hollowed look and robbing her of femininity. The shadows in the room pronounced the wrinkles about her eyes and mouth. She bent over an old, finely polished, secretary's desk with a glass hutch above. Ledger pages lay before her.

Rebecca approached, downing the last of the juice in her cup and grimaced.

"Oh, that is nasty," Rebecca said.

"Doctor's orders," Eva said.

"May I speak with you, Madam Eva?" Rebecca asked timidly, approaching the secretary's desk.

Sporting the same uniform, it didn't degrade her grace and charm like it did Eva. Rebecca's platinum blond hair fell in long waves, cascading past her neck and down her shoulders. Her eyes sparkled and she glowed with an elegant beauty from a time past.

"What now?" Eva sighed with frustration.

"With the master's arrival," Rebecca said. "I was hoping you'd suggest what we talked about at dinner the other night, about the cross-training and benefits of education for some of the staff? You could present it as a cost savings, and he may see the value of investing in the staff already working here."

Rebecca stepped forward and slipped a brochure on the desk.

"The local college has adult classes for auto and appliance repair, and Carmichael has voiced an interest."

"If you feel so strongly about it," Eva snipped. "Why don't you bring it up to the master yourself?"

"I would never presume to …," Rebecca said. "I mean, I won't over step you."

"Alright, I'll bring it up if the opportunity presents itself." Eva glared at her over her readers. "Is that all?"

"The windows."

"Not the windows again, Becca. I know they leak in the winter."

"Yes, but I saw this in a magazine." Rebecca slid another paper before Eva. "We hire a company to repair and clean them several times a year. With new windows we could cut our heating and cooling costs down, and with the way they fold in, we can wash them ourselves from inside the house. We'd save money."

"You do realize that you're creating more work for those in the house?" said Eva. "That doesn't make you very popular."

"I'm just trying to help. Remember the old days when we'd drag the carpets out and beat them? Now we have vacuum cleaners. We used to wash clothes by hand, but now we have machines. I'm just saying we have the time to do it, and it's not like we're hanging off the roof to wash them."

"I'll think about …." Eva began but was interrupted by the bell above the door. "The master is here. Is his room ready?"

"Yes, Madam," Rebecca said.

"Good." Eva rose from the desk and pushed her chair in. "His flights are usually grueling, and he'll want to rest before the Crumbs. His schedule is aggressive and won't afford him long to linger here. I heard he's due back in London, and then Stockholm by early next week."

"Yes, Madam." Rebecca followed quickly. "Why can't I be a housekeeper and stay in the kitchen? No one will miss me."

"You can't hide in the kitchen forever."

"But I'm not like the rest."

"You're no different than anyone else in this house. Now come along. And don't dawdle," Eva said. "And you don't want him to see you at work, so keep a low profile while he's here and promptly leave if he enters a room while you're cleaning. Unlike children, the staff are *neither* to be seen *nor* heard."

"Yes, Madam Eva."

Eva walked quickly. When she headed straight for the front door, Rebecca turned the corner. Her mind drifted for only a moment on how peaceful the kitchen would be this time of day. Without thinking, she started in that direction. Then, catching herself, Rebecca twisted, adjusted her path, and caught up to Eva.

"Where do you think you were going?" Eva scolded. "It is the habit of the master to greet the staff. It may be just a formality, but he is very ritualistic. And his suckling will hold off his cravings. Come on, hurry."

Rebecca stood in line as others arrived. The staff for this house numbered around thirty. She took her place at the end of the line and fixated her eyes on the plush carpet immediately before her. Eva stood beside Timothy, the new butler, at the front near the entranceway. And new in the manor was a relative term. Timothy was brought from England in 1945 where he shadowed the London butler for a year.

Several other staff members stood between Rebecca and Eva, one being the gardener, a few valets, and another housekeeper like herself. New to the housekeeping department, Rebecca wished she could avoid this part of it, dreading the thought of the suckling. She preferred her anonymity in the kitchen.

Gretta, one of the kitchen staff, snuck up to the doorway

across from Rebecca. She waved, catching Rebecca's wandering eye. She smiled at Gretta who whispered, "Good luck" and gave her two thumbs up. Rebecca shyly smiled back and nodded. Then another housekeeper moved to her side.

"Don't look so nervous," Elizabeth said. "Breathe before you pass out."

Rebecca inhaled and slowly released it.

"Don't let Eva scare you. Lord Englewood will come in, talk to a few of us, perhaps suckle, and then move on. Then we'll be allowed to return to our jobs. Madam says you don't like the suckling?"

"No," Rebecca said.

"We, at this end, don't get it every time. Relax, it'll be over very soon."

As Rebecca looked at the familiar faces, they all seemed excited and shared attractive appearances. None were flawed by moles, bad teeth, thinning hair, or misshapen noses. None were heavy, too tall, or too short.

To Rebecca, the gathering looked more like a gaggle of models waiting to pose for the cover of a magazine. Even Eva was well proportioned and attractive for her age. All the women held themselves with grace and a look of superiority, while the men stood proud and strong. But Rebecca didn't feel pretty or desirable. She was damaged, which weighed on her even if the others didn't care.

The house was made up of a strange lot of people. Some were pre-America having come over from Europe as colonists and of great age, or like Madam Eva, during the Revolutionary War. Some from times in between wars and some as recent as WWI and II. For the most part, they remained in their groups. During socials, some of the men bickered as to which wars had the most casualties or saw more action. The younger males' conversations reverted to automobiles and how they ranked through the decades. The women usually gathered like chickens in a henhouse, comparing lives and lovers or gossiping about movie stars.

The door opened and Rebecca held her breath, but Carmichael, the chauffeur, entered carrying an overnight bag and larger suitcase. The next was a valet who held the master's briefcase. They both led the way and disappeared down the hall, but not before she recognized the marks of suckling on them.

Lord Devlin Englewood stepped in the door, tall and lean, wearing reflective shades and dressed in a tan Savile Row suit. His wind-whipped hair lay in waves down past his ears and onto his collar. Rebecca hadn't seen him in years because the kitchen staff weren't required for this awkward meet and greet.

She watched as Devlin paused before the first few servants. The women offered a shallow curtsy while the men nodded a bow. They spoke briefly and quietly, and Devlin smiled, intently focused. Then he removed his sunglasses and leaned toward each on the far side of their faces where she couldn't see. But she knew what he did.

Eva approached Devlin with Timothy, the butler, a slender, smartly dressed man, who took Devlin's coat and shades. Rebecca's curiosity got the better of her, and she met Devlin's glance, but quickly returned her gaze to the carpet. Nervous, flushed with mixed feelings, Rebecca prepared herself for her turn before the lord of the manor.

"Thank you, Timothy," Devlin addressed the butler. "It's very good to see you."

"Welcome back, sir," Timothy replied. "How are those on the isle?"

"Well, and they ask after you often."

"I'm pleased to hear that. I hope your flight was uneventful."

"Yes, uneventful, just long and frustrating."

"I can imagine," Timothy replied.

Devlin leaned in as he had done before. Timothy's body flinched, then slouched as he breathed an audible sigh of relief. He stepped out around Devlin and disappeared into another room. Rebecca glanced back at the others who smiled with dumbfounded expressions.

"Your room is ready, Lord Devlin," Eva said.

"Thank you, Eva," Devlin replied with a hint of fatigue. "And the special delivery...?"

"Yes, that has been arranged. Everything as you requested."

"Excellent," Devlin said.

Eva nodded.

Devlin's fancy European shoes stopped before Rebecca. Starting to curtsy, she lost her balance. Devlin extended his hand and steadied her as she resumed her full height. Unable to keep her eyes downcast, her heart raced and her palms sweated.

She met his glance. Handsome and as youthful looking as ever, except for his bloodshot eyes. And Rebecca realized she had waited too long to look upon his face. How she missed seeing him.

"Lord Devlin," Rebecca mumbled. "Welcome."

He leaned over her but not like he did to the others, and his chin was level with her ear.

"I can smell your fear, beautiful, but it is unfounded." Devlin's velvet voice sent chills up her arms. "Be at peace."

Rebecca smiled slightly, but the nervousness didn't abate.

"Are you always this graceful?" he asked with a smirk. "Do I know you?"

Rebecca heard Eva grinding her teeth in displeasure, assuming her lack of gracefulness the reason.

"She's new to housekeeping," Eva explained. "Reassigned from the kitchen."

"And your name?" Devlin asked.

Rebecca's mouth instantly dried, and her throat croaked. "Reb—Becca Bellows, sir."

"Becca? Not the name I would think of an angel, but just as beautiful as I'd imagined one to be," Devlin replied.

His hand lifted her chin and moved it from side to side. Her hair fell away from her neck.

"When were you suckled last? I see your marks are healed."

An unconscious reaction, she reached for her neck. "A while," she replied timidly. "And it was by one of your family when they visited last."

"May I?" he asked. She nodded.

Rebecca turned, exposing her neck, but as she felt him near, she flinched. And a slight tremble moved through her body. Devlin stopped immediately.

"You're afraid of this?" he asked. "Or you don't like it, perhaps?"

"Not really," Rebecca replied. "Others say it's euphoric, but I don't feel it, and it gives me a headache lasting for a week."

"That's strange," Devlin said. "But not necessary, I've had my fill."

Devlin walked past Rebecca with Eva on his heels. But Rebecca knew she would feel Eva's coarse reprimand once they were alone for her ungraceful distraction of the master. One day Eva caught Rebecca in the master's library, and since then, Eva had taken it upon herself to harass Rebecca on every minor issue. Rebecca believed it was jealousy on Eva's part because Eva could barely read. Eva's distrust of her and micromanaging reminded Rebecca she wasn't Eva's favorite employee.

But in a small way, Rebecca relished in Devlin's momentary attention. He always smelled of the best colognes and wore the finest clothes. He was kind and lavish to his employees, but he never visited this home for long. Once a month, he arrived, and all the servants talked of him and excitedly anticipated his stay. Rebecca didn't share in that excitement and hid from him. It wasn't that she disliked or feared him, but her life was irrelevant to his, and there was peace in the status quo.

Chapter 6

The Crumbs from the Master's Table

That evening, as the staff gathered eagerly on the back steps that led to the dungeon, Rebecca waited on the upper staircase. She knew only a little of what happens when the master resided at this location but never felt worthy to attend. 'Crumbs from the Master's Table' the servants called it, but Rebecca knew no crumbs were involved. Having caught Devlin's notice, she longed to see more of him again, even if it meant being a witness to this event.

Having been part of the kitchen staff, Rebecca usually volunteered to prep the kitchen for the next day during these events. She didn't mind not attending and felt she contributed to the household. A loner most of the time, she minded her own business and tried to avoid the staff's dramas as much as possible. She had her friends who had urged her to attend "the Crumbs" with them, but had always declined.

The staff descended the two flights to the dungeon in an enthusiastic forum. Their voices were eager and joyous, and it drew her. This was a party the master opened to the staff, and they seemed very appreciative of it. All of them dressed to the nines. Rebecca relied on the staff for their hand-me-downs for her clothes and felt very underdressed as she followed. Even Eva attended in a black floor-length gown with sequins. Rebecca figured Eva oversaw the event to ensure no one exceeded their limit or stepped out of line.

What a drag, going to a party with a wet blanket like her. Who wants to attend a party with your boss anyway? But Devlin saw me, and I'd give anything to catch his eye again.

Rebecca crept behind the crowd, lingering conspicuously a level above. They moved quickly once at the base of the stairs, and so did she. The room before the dungeon was empty of soft furnishings with a marble sepulcher in the middle raised by one large slab of granite. Barely lit, torches held by ornate metal fixtures left only enough light to travel through the room. The Shadows the other's cast played tricks with her eyes, which slowed her from following.

The walls looked like sandstone, but perfectly rounded and smooth. This outer room's acoustics were painful to her ears, so she hurried through to the pocket doors on the far side and hid in the shadows. Vague memories flashed in her mind from the night she had arrived. The sound of this door moving when Devlin carried her here had not changed, grinding like a great weight.

I shouldn't be here. I'm not like the others; I feel as if I'm intruding—but he noticed me. I'm so stupid to think he would again. I should just go…

The voices grew as she neared the stone vertical slabs of marble. In the center of the room, under the spotlight, stood a stainless-steel table. The one she remembered was a white porcelain pedestal table, and new in its day. The image had been burned into her memory from the trauma of the event. She recalled thinking how the white molded porcelain held a sort of pure beauty, at least until Doctor Wells operated on her. Then the table, the room, and events that unfolded after became a horrid reminder of how her life had changed. Avoiding the dungeon since then had given her a semblance of peace.

The room had changed greatly since she had seen it. The white porcelain table had been replaced by a stainless steel one, no less shiny, with a sink faucet and basin at the end. A four-inch raised lip surrounded it and a man lay still within its walls. Another modification to the table had been wrist and ankle cuffs welded to the frame.

The man on the table had straps across his chest, gagged and his wrists and ankles in the metal cuffs. Motionless, he looked already dead. His orange jumpsuit glowed under the bright fluorescent troffers. His clothes had been cut to expose his arms and legs. Hanging from the table was a tube with a clamp to keep it closed. Entering the doors, she took notice to it all and quickly moved to the back wall, away from everyone.

Between her and the staff were folding chairs arranged as if a small play was about to be performed before the mortuary table. But no one sat. They congregated in their groups, talking as if this was a social hour at the local garden club. Rarely did Rebecca see Eva smile as much as she did tonight. The woman beamed, speaking casually, and laughing. Many of the others held beautiful goblets. Carmichael looked dashing in his tux.

Elizabeth waved Rebecca to join her, but Rebecca shook her head and pressed herself against the back wall. Even Carmichael winked at her. They accepted her willingly, but her own feeling of inadequacy separated her from her friends. Men died in the dungeon, but Rebecca knew little else. She trembled slightly and not because the dungeon was chilly.

In the background, Rebecca spied Devlin hovering over the body. He was shirtless, pale and without blemish, and she couldn't look away. She knew he was ancient compared to her, yet he looked no more than mid-twenties. He winked at the staff who responded to him and gave him their attention.

Devlin stood over the man. Then slapped his face to awaken him. The man moved sluggishly as Devlin resumed his seat and took a manilla folder. He waited on the prisoner to continue.

"For the crimes of rape and murder, you lay before us," Devlin said.

Devlin pushed the shackled man's head to the side. The voices and movement of the staff stilled. Rebecca could tell by Devlin's smile, which revealed two long canine-like fangs, that he made eye contact with the staff, and their eagerness encouraged him. Then Devlin opened his mouth. The pristine white fangs caught the light, and he dove on the man's exposed neck.

The body jolted and stiffened. Then the man awoke and began to thrash, but the restraints held. His body twisted wildly with an ear-shattering scream. Devlin didn't let go, and blood splattered and flew around him.

Rebecca covered her ears and lost sight of the table, the prisoner, and Devlin as the staff circled like vultures. They cheered and celebrated something beyond her sight. She dragged a folding chair to the wall and climbed above the crowd to see Devlin and the prisoner again.

Devlin rose with blood on his chin and running down his chest. Even as gruesome a sight as this, Devlin remained handsome. He stepped back, withdrew a long silver scalpel, then cut the arms and ankles of the man as the others hovered closer. Now Rebecca understood the purpose of the mortuary table. It collected the blood and the tube at the end turned dark as it filled.

Carmichael stepped forward first, placing his goblet under the tube and release the clamp to catch the crimson flow. Then, one by one, the staff did the same with their goblets as casually as if it had been beer. Except Eva, she didn't partake, though she witnessed it all with a smile and nod to the others.

Rebecca froze with bewilderment, more curiosity than fear. She remembered Tony had been strapped to a vertical table, no longer in the room, a wooden rack used for torture. She assumed Tony's fate had been the same as this prisoner. It had never bothered her before and still didn't.

Stunned, Rebecca couldn't move at first, but soon, the smell of the blood permeated the air like a thick curtain. Her stomach wrenched. She covered her mouth; afraid she'd toss dinner. Her eyes met Devlin's, and he gave her a curious gaze in return. Then she felt an overwhelming fear as if intruding in a restricted area. She leapt from the chair and ran from the room, leaving the laughter and merriment behind. Unhindered, she didn't stop until she slammed the door to her bedroom on the uppermost floor of the house.

Traffic watching always calmed her. As dusk turned to night and the street lights took over for the sun, her mind rehearsed the scene. Like some twisted reality, she didn't struggle, but accept it. But whether she knew it before or not, Lord Devlin was not what he seemed.

But what of the others?

***

The following day, still reeling from the night's horror, Rebecca joined the others for breakfast. She watched them closely; they ate regular food. None appeared to have fangs or acted outside of the socially accepted norms. They all behaved as their usual selves, albeit slightly more cheerful. The one thing she thought odd, no one spoke of the event.

Rebecca completed her morning chores early and headed to her bedroom when she heard Eva at the door of Devlin's study. Eva entered, and the door closed. Rebecca crept to the landing outside the study and could hear them plainly from the stairs.

"You wanted to speak to me concerning the staff," Devlin said. "I, too, need to bring up a subject that concerns me. I will address your concerns first."

"Yes, Lord Devlin," Eva paused. "One of the staff has voiced an interest in taking an adult education course in auto repair. Another servant wishes to learn plumbing and handy-man skills."

"What do you propose?" asked Devlin.

"With your permission, an education budget."

"How much are we talking about?"

"I'm not sure. It would depend on the courses, I guess." Eva replied.

"It sounds like…" Devlin paused. "A good idea. Having in-house workers would be a cost benefit and decrease the need for outside contractors, wouldn't it? The less people who know what happens here, the better."

Oh my God, he liked my ideas?

"Yes, exactly," Eva faltered. "And the windows, sir."

"Windows?"

"These windows are very drafty in the winter, and we employ outside help to maintain them. If we changed them out for new, thermal panes as you see there." Rebecca assumed Eva showed him the advertisement. "We could potentially remove the need for outside companies as well."

"Again, making this an in-house chore?" Devlin asked. "I like it. Can you shop this for me, work up a few estimates for the next time I'm here?"

"Yes, sir, most happily," Eva said.

"Now to my business, I need to pull Timothy and Roger, the gardener, for the London estate. I've just lost two good men, and since this lawn is the size of a postage stamp and I'm rarely here, I thought it better to move some around instead of bringing in from outside."

"I'm sure they both will be eager for the change," Eva stuttered. "We'll make do without them."

"Excellent." Devlin moved causing his chair to squeak. "My other concern is this Miss Bellows. Tell me about her."

A cold panic rushed through Rebecca's veins.

"What specifically do you want to know?" Eva replied.

"How loyal is she? The suckle marks on her neck are healed."

"Completely loyal," Eva replied without any hesitation. "I find no fault in her in that area."

"Familiars live for the venom. If not suckled, why is she so loyal?"

"She's not a Familiar, not like the rest of them. More like me, your humble and loyal servant."

What is a Familiar?

"How did she come to be here?"

"You saved her life. And for it, she vowed her life's service to you."

"When did I do that?" he asked.

"Sometime between the First and Second World Wars, I can't remember how every servant came to be with us."

"Why don't I see her wages in the accounting?" he asked.

"She refuses to take them," Eva said. "She doesn't want to be a burden and feels her room and board are more than enough. She's been content with this situation for decades. I'm surprised you didn't notice it before now."

"I didn't notice her before now," Devlin said. "And how are her work habits?"

"She's one of my best."

You could've fooled me, old nag. Never a kind word and talk about hovering.

"Fast, efficient, follows orders, and quite competent," Eva continued. "That's why I felt it was time to bring her out of the kitchen."

"Outside interests?"

"I don't know of any."

"No hobbies? Is she involved perhaps with someone on staff?"

"Lord," Eva said. "This is a huge house with many hands. I can't be expected to know everyone intimately."

Geez, I eat meals with her every day. How much more exposure does she need? She knows exactly how I arrived here. She's lying for me, why?

"What I do know is she's shy and enjoys reading," Eva continued. "I find her here on sunny days with her nose pressed in a book while the others go out. Why are you worried?"

"Anyone content here with no outside interests is peculiar, especially if they aren't a Familiar," Devlin said. "What is she hiding from?"

"Sir, when she came to us, she was – a broken woman." Eva's voice reflected a momentary warmth. "Life hadn't been kind to her, and what she suffered took a long while to recover from, but she has found peace here. She is valued and appreciated by many."

"But for how long?" Devlin asked. "And the fact that she doesn't suckle or join in with "the Crumbs" makes me think she's hiding some motive to be here that is not all pure. Like maybe she was sent here to spy on us."

"If she had just arrived, I might agree. But she's been here a long time."

These people have become like family. Where would I go if I did leave?

"Yes, she has proven herself in that regard," Devlin said. "I feel like I should know her, yet I can't remember it."

"Lord Devlin, if you're so worried, speak to her."

Oh, God, no. His arrival and last night was embarrassing enough for a while. Probably trip all over myself again and look like a bigger fool than I already do.

"Find out her motives for yourself," Eva continued. "She's smart, content, and it was she who has made the suggestions concerning the improvements I brought to you. But like all of us here, she has a past that has darkened her soul. Timid, reserved, perhaps even boring, but she's normal for us. She may not participate as the others, but she's accepted as one of us."

Why is she standing up for me? I thought she hated me.

"Last night," Devlin said. "Her actions during the Crumbs indicated as if one was witnessing it for the first time."

"The opportunity to bring her from the kitchen wasn't only

because I needed her as a housekeeper. She has a bad reaction to blood. Our accident-prone chef cuts himself often, and she becomes useless for the rest of the shift. I thought, by bringing her up the ladder, I was helping her. And she's what they call now "cross-trained". Making her even more valuable as a servant."

"An aversion toward blood?" Devlin asked. "That would explain her reaction. But why now, if she's been here many years, did she attend?"

"I'm not sure."

"What if this new revelation causes her to want to leave my employment?"

"She has given no indication of that before. And seemed normal this morning."

"But she knows what happens in the dungeon now."

"And I think she already knew. But seeing it first-hand can be a bit of a shock. If I had any doubts, I'd have vocalize them to you. But I'll watch her to see if last night changed her in any way. But I don't think it did, not by her reaction this morning. She seemed – unaffected."

"I hope you're right," Devlin said.

"If she's fine with it, why try to fix something that's not broken?"

"You're right, Madam," Devlin said. Rebecca could hear the creak in the chair as he reclined. "This is why I trust you. You know my house, protect it with your life, and you give me sound wisdom. I'll leave this in your capable hands until I hear differently from you.

But you know, no one ever leaves my employment—alive."

"Yes, sir."

"Work up those estimates on the windows. I'm interested to see how much the initial costs compare to the long-term savings. And as far as the education budget, as long as it does not exceed ten thousand a year, I'll approve it."

"That is very generous."

"I believe in education. And surprised any Familiar would even consider it."

"Yes, sir," Eva said.

Rebecca moved up stairs quickly before being found. Their conversation left her with some trepidation as to not being able to ever leave. In all the decades she had worked for the master, that had never been communicated to her before. And she pondered it.

Chapter 7

The Master

A day had passed since Rebecca eavesdropped on Lord Devlin's conversation with Eva. She meditated on Eva's compliments and allowed herself to enjoy them, despite Eva's continued scrutiny of her work. Eva's contentions were unabated, as if the conversation never happened.

It's her job to make sure I work hard. I'll stop taking it so personal. And as to what happened in the dungeon, I don't have to partake to be here. Eva didn't and she's accepted.

Rebecca snuck to the library, perched in the window, and cracked open a book. Not a best-seller, but it kept her attention. This was her idea of time well spent, the sun, a book, and hours to be engrossed in anything other than the house drama.

The warm sunlight chased away the lingering coldness that never entirely left her body. The doctors attributed the lack of circulation in her hands and legs to the long-term effects of the fevers. But other than that, she had regained her looks and stamina with the help of the tomato juice.

Not used to the master being about, Rebecca neglected to

close the library door. Had she done so, she would have heard it open. Instead, out of the corner of her eye, she spotted Devlin leaning against the doorframe, still in his pajamas and house coat with his arms folded across his chest. Startled, she snapped the book closed.

"I'm sorry, I'll go," Rebecca said, about to launch from the window seat.

"No, stay." Devlin crossed the room. "I just needed something from my desk. But I didn't want to disturb you. You were so quiet and peaceful, like the dead. You like that window to read in?"

"Yes," she replied.

"I thought you'd be with the others watching TV or going to the local pub?"

"I prefer reading to TV."

"Me too," Devlin said. "I like to read downstairs. Now, where is that letter – here it is."

Rebecca opened her book, but her gaze followed him. When he looked back up, their eyes met, and she offered a polite smile. But Devlin didn't break the hold and wandered closer, almost shyly.

"I'm bored," he announced. "Would you join me for a movie at a theater? I take it you're not working now, are you?"

Me? Is this his way to get to know me? If I decline, he might get suspicious and question my loyalty again. What would be the harm of one movie? It's not a bar, and he's not a gangster. No, he's a vampire, but which would be worse?

"No," she replied. "If I still worked in the kitchen, I would. But I'm done for the day."

"Good, let's go."

"Madam Eva wouldn't approve." Rebecca rose and hugged the book against her chest. "She discourages me from going out after what happened to me. I've gone to the pub with the other staff a few times. It always ends badly."

"How so?"

"Men try to pick me up," she replied. "Usually, one or more of the male servant's sport bruises from defending me. I've never found a generation that respects the word no. Madam Eva says the streets aren't as safe as they used to be. But they weren't all that safe back in my day, either. So, to keep the others from harm, I stay home."

"But everyone could use a little danger in their lives." He smiled devilishly. "I can protect you better than they could. Do you want to see a movie?"

"Yes, sir," she replied eagerly. "It would be nice to get away."

"Or it's me and not the movie you hesitate with?"

"Not you, sir." Rebecca felt embarrassed and nodded. "Alright. As long as the Madam doesn't find out."

"Great. Meet me out front. I'll ring for the car. And I guess I should get dressed."

The 1960 silver Rolls Royce Phantom pulled up out front, and Rebecca waited patiently. Devlin soon appeared, closing the front door dressed in faded jeans and a pink polo shirt. It seemed strange to Rebecca to see him in casual clothes, especially as outdated as those from the 80s.

Carmichael opened the door and gave her a strange look as she entered. Devlin waited, then joined her in the back seat. He kept to his side. The Rolls pulled up to the curb and they were dropped off at the front of the theater. As a gentleman, Devlin offered his arm. Rebecca took it as he led her to the ticket counter. Even out front, the waves of buttery popcorn scents wafted past them. Devlin asked if she wanted something to eat, but she declined.

They found their seats, and the show began. The trumpets blared as the MGM lion appeared. The sound startled her, and she jumped in her seat. She felt a hand on her arm.

"Are you alright?" Devlin asked.

"It's just so loud," she said.

"Yes, I'm sensitive to it too. Here." He handed her a small plastic bag with two fluorescent foam ear plugs. Then she noticed he had them as well. She quickly tore open the baggy and set them in her ears.

"The screen is huge," Rebecca said. "Madam used to send the others out to rent movies until the store closed. Now they are all on DVD's, whatever those are. But the TV at the house has nothing on this."

"Wait till you see the special effects."

"What are those?"

"You'll see."

Midway through the first scene, Rebecca leaned over to Devlin.

"Is that what space really looks like?" she asked.

"I don't know, I haven't been there," he replied with a coy smile.

"I heard we went to the moon. Is that real?"

"Yes, I guess so."

"Is this real," she asked.

"No, this is make-believe. They call it science fiction."

"I saw some of those books on your shelves. I thought they were science books. I'll have to take a second look."

"You'll find this movie among them," Devlin said.

"In one of my magazines, it said that this movie had five rotten tomatoes. Is that good or bad?"

"Watch the movie and decide for yourself. I don't go by what others say."

"Have you read Tolkien?" Rebecca asked.

"Yes, my precious," Devlin replied with a slur. "Have you seen the movie?"

"They made a movie out of the set of books?" Rebecca asked so innocently. "That must be an ungodly long movie."

Devlin burst with a chuckle that drew some unwanted attention. He seemed so natural, honest, and comfortable. It calmed her trepidation and removed her shyness. He slid down in his seat, and she did the same.

"They made three different movies," Devlin whispered.

"They call them a trilogy."

"What'll they think of next?" Rebecca replied. "And it's in color. It's beautiful and bright."

"You're beautiful," Devlin replied. Their eyes met.

"I used to be." Rebecca returned to sitting straight. "Most of the others in the house are better looking."

"Beauty is in the eye of the beholder," Devlin said.

After another half hour, Rebecca was engrossed in the cinematography and story when she felt something on her shoulder. She found his arm resting on the back of her seat, and his fingers grazed her skin. Distracted, she glanced over, but he seemed as engrossed as she had been.

The male sex hasn't changed since I dated last. How long has it been since I was out on a date? Sixty, seventy years—damn, over eighty years. I wonder if he'll want me to "put out" at the end of the evening. Never dawned on me he'd want that. Tony sure did. But I'm old. True, but he's older. I wonder how old is Lord Devlin?

His hand moved again, more noticeable than before. She reached for it, interlocking her fingers in his. Then, very casually, she smiled at his slightly stunned, questioning face. The corner of his lips tilted up, and his eyes returned to the screen.

What in the hell am I doing holding hands with a...? But nothing about him screams.... He's sweet, boyishly charming, and handsome. Well, they say that about serial killers, too.

Returning her attention to the screen, Rebecca leaned closer to him, knowing he acknowledged her invitation. This ensured he would not grab for any place indecent, so she enjoyed the rest of the movie. They held hands in the car in the dark, but he never made another advance.

When they arrived home, Devlin escorted her into the house and up the first flight of stairs near his study. Rebecca stood on one step above him; only slightly taller. She felt him hesitate.

"Thank you," Rebecca said. "I really enjoyed it. I didn't think I would. The last time I was in a movie theater, the movies were black and white."

"You're welcome," Devlin replied. "I enjoyed your company. Maybe while I'm here…"

Rebecca heard the door to the kitchen swing open. The footfalls she recognized.

Madam Eva is coming from the kitchen.

"I'd better get to bed," Rebecca said. She wanted to kiss him on the cheek, but he turned his head just as she neared, kissing him briefly on the lips. It startled her, and he returned a look of surprise. But Eva was coming and she didn't have time to explain. "Thank you, again."

And she dashed up the stairs.

"But…?" Devlin called after her.

From above, Rebecca noticed Devlin touch his lips where they connected. He glanced up, and their eyes met. She smiled back. But knowing Eva was about to appear, she backed away from the rail. Devlin had just left her sight when Rebecca heard Eva address Lord Devlin a good night.

by K.A. Monaco

That was close.

Chapter 8

Resumption

Three days had passed since Devlin's arrival. Special deliveries may have arrived, but Rebecca took no notice of it. She had turned a blind eye to them before, and with Devlin's attention, she felt the Crumbs and what the staff did with them were none of her business.

Eva hadn't mentioned that she knew Rebecca had gone out with Lord Devlin and Rebecca assumed she didn't know. But wisdom told Rebecca that Eva was not stupid and would reprimand her if caught with the master. Still, it was hard to keep the smile from her face. She floated through her day thinking about the kiss. In a way, it had been stolen, but he didn't indicate displeasure or acceptance. She began to wonder.

Dusting a sitting room off the master suite, Rebecca paused to look out the second-story window at Central Park. That morning, she had awoken in a pool of sweat after dreams of the night she met Devlin. Perhaps a visit to the dungeon had provoked her memories. Though she didn't dream often, her past had been a blur. But on the occasion a recollection returned, she wrote it down.

Standing in the sunlight, she closed her eyes. She returned to dream; the basement bar in the Bronx. It was the Speakeasy Tony and his gang frequented during Prohibition. The warm ground against the cool October rain ad produced patches of fog that laid at street level, but only visible under the street lights. Tony had dragged her out to the loading docks behind the brick building.

"I told you, bitch," Tony yelled, with a thick New York accent, then slapped her hard. "No one cheats on me."

"But it was just a dance." Rebecca remembered how her cheek burned.

"No," Tony replied. "Not the way he looked at you and you looked at him. You've been seeing each other behind my back."

"Tony, you know I work all day and spend my nights with you," she said. "When do I have time to cheat?"

Tony slapped her again.

At least it was his back hand, hitting the opposite cheek. It didn't hurt as much as the first time. Oh, how I wish I could break up with him, but our family needs the money. His rage deafens him to logic and common sense. What am I doing with this asshole? She remembered thinking.

"Don't talk back to me!"

"You shouldn't hit women," a voice from behind her said with a distinct English accent.

Rebecca knew it was the man she tangoed with who angered Tony. She did not turn to see him but saw the flash of light reflected off the chrome of Tony's pistol.

"You!" Tony raised the pistol, but turned to address

Rebecca. "So, if you ain't cheatin' on me? And he means nothin'?
Then killen' him ain't gonna mean nothin' either."

"No!" Rebecca grabbed the gun and forced it to point at the
ground between them, but Tony was taller and stronger than her,
pulling it back up. The sound that followed was like the pop of a cork
under pressure. The sensation of the burn and pain that followed
made her gasp. Tony's fire arm had discharged.

She stood in shock when a hand grabbed her shoulder and
pushed her to the side. She stumbled and clutched at the wall as she
fell to her knees. Some dark shadow stood between her and Tony.
She couldn't make out the form of the figure or the words they
exchanged, but the sweet pronunciation of each syllable revealed
who it was.

Rebecca jumped as she remembered it, breaking her
concentration. Quickly, she withdrew her manuscript, flipped to the
proper part, and began scribbling what she recalled in the margins.
She ran the scene through her mind again while fresh, yet her body
sweated under the trauma from the vivid memory. She focused on
her writing when movement near the pocket doors startled her.

Madam Eva's most explicit and repeated instructions were
not to disturb or hinder the Master. Not seen nor heard.

Rebecca headed for the hallway, slipping the papers down the
front of her apron and into the pocket. The house had a myriad of
sliding pocket doors, and as she fled, the one leading to the bedroom
slid open. And there he was, as handsome as the night before.
Flustered, she dropped her gaze and raced for the grand stairway.

Her feet carried her quickly down the plush, carpeted stairs to the laundry room.

She rounded the corner when she felt for the papers that should have been in her pocket but were missing. This wasn't the first time she had missed the pocket and they fell, so she checked all her pockets, hoping she just misplaced them. Retracing her steps wasn't necessary either; she knew exactly where they lay, by the window in the sitting room. Panic filled her heart, and she only hoped she could recover them before he found them.

Though she tried to focus on folding the linens, she fretted for a long hour before Eva turned the corner.

"There you are," Eva said with a scolding tone to her voice. Her gruffness superseded her pleasant attitude with Rebecca. "The master asked to see you."

"Did he say why?" Rebecca asked, but she knew.

"No, but I'm sure you did something wrong," Eva said. "Come along. You don't want to keep him waiting."

Rebecca assumed a reprimand was coming, first from the master, then Eva, and worse than the first time she caught the master's attention. Rebecca followed Eva back up to the master suite. Each step took an extra effort, and her heart sank. Eva opened the pocket doors, and Rebecca stepped through and advanced. But then she heard the door again. Eva closed them from the opposite side. Rebecca realized she faced the master alone.

Humbly, she pressed closer to the sofa in the sitting room where Devlin sat. Without acknowledging her, he raised his hand,

and waved her to draw near. The day half gone, Rebecca noticed Devlin still dressed in his house coat and pajamas.

She recognized her papers in his hands and a hot flash gripped her as her ears began to burn. She advanced slowly, apprehensively. He ran his fingers through his hair, then flipped one of the pages. He read them diligently.

Oh, God, what if he remembers? I'm not sure I'm ready...

"I can still smell your fear, child," he said, and their eyes caught. "You have no reason for it. Come in, Becca, sit down." His voice lacked any malice or coarseness.

"Madam won't let us sit on the furnishings where you reside," Rebecca said.

"Am I not the master here?" He held out his hand and pointed to the seat beside him.

"Yes, sir. As you wish." Rebecca sat gingerly on the tapestry settee, poised to leap to her feet at any moment.

"Where did you come upon these?" he asked.

"I wrote them." Rebecca stared at the floral pattern on the rug before her.

"You?" Devlin paused. "You wrote this?"

"Yes," Rebecca said sheepishly. "I'd like to have them back, please. No one is meant to see them. Madam Eva will be quite cross to find out..."

"She won't find out from me." He paused. "It's quite good. I enjoyed it. Is it a true story?"

"Based on true events. Names changed to protect the

innocent, and I embellish a bit."

"It's a romance?"

"Yes."

"Where did you learn to write like this?"

"Just by reading books from your library. I read a lot, and that came out of me."

"You're proud of it?" The way he casually spoke calmed some of her fears while distracting her as well.

"Amazed I wrote it." Rebecca slouched and leaned against the back of the settee. "When I came here, I was almost illiterate."

"You've been adding to it recently? The pencil here is fresh."

"Yes, as I remember things," Rebecca stuttered.

"Where did we meet?" he asked. He lifted the manuscript. "I can't recall. Yet I feel like I should know you. Is this how we met?"

Rebecca hesitated. This was the moment she dreaded for decades. Had the feelings she felt been one sided. Or did he forget her like a bad night of drinking.

"Hhhmmm?" he persisted.

"Yes, a speakeasy," she said reluctantly. "In October of 1928."

"Refresh my memory," he said with a smile. "Which parts are embellished and which aren't?"

"The antagonist was a guy by the name of Tony Parker, but he liked his nickname – Tony Too Tall. In those days, you couldn't toss a rock without hitting a gagster. That place was where all the other gangsters socialized."

"And the protagonist was his girlfriend?" Devlin asked. She felt his eyes burrowing into her flesh.

"Yes. Along came this British fellow who kept her company for a bit. Tony never liked it when his gal talked to other men. Even if it was just in passing. He took her out back of the joint and started beating her."

"The protagonist was you?" Devlin asked.

Rebecca nodded reluctantly.

This is where it becomes dicey.

"Tony accused the Brit—well, me of cheating on him. He demanded to know who the man was," Rebecca replied. "I didn't know, and he didn't believe me. Said you were watching me all night and that we didn't look like strangers. I tried to explain, but he didn't want to hear it."

"Why were you with a man like that?"

She thought for a moment. So much time had passed. "My father was injured in WWI, and my mother worked two jobs. All my brothers and sisters were too young to help. By day, I worked at the Woolworths down on Nineth Street. I met Tony one day while working and he invited me out. He didn't seem bad at first and he let me keep the change from the drinks he bought. I was taking two dollars a night home just in his pocket change. That was enough to feed my entire family for a week. My mother didn't know what he was like but encouraged me to go out with him because of the money. But I had my own ambitions. I used to see the women from the steno pool come in to purchase their nylons and makeup. They were so fashionable and independent. I wanted to be like them, but there was no way I could land a job like that."

"How did you come to be here?"

"When Tony hit me," she said. "You suddenly appeared. You rescued me from him, saved my life, and brought me here."

"I'm sorry I can't remember it. Was that the first time he hurt you?"

"No, the night before he ripped my dress when he…he had unspoken expectations. I wanted to leave him after that, but Tony wasn't the kind of guy you get rid of easily."

"So, I brought you here. What happened to your boyfriend?"

"The same thing that happened in the basement the other night, I presume. Some parts I don't want to remember." Rebecca looked away. "After that night, my memory is segmented. I write in case I forget again."

Remembering how Tony had taken advantage brought up feelings of shame and embarrassment. Rebecca had not realized how low she had stooped for her family.

Devlin nodded and scooted over to her. "You're courageous and honest; that's rare—I like it."

"I figured if you asked," she said. "Then you must want to know the truth."

Devlin smiled and leaned in her direction. "You figured right."

As he approached, she slid into the corner of the sofa.

"About that kiss…" Devlin gazed upon her face.

"I should go," Rebecca said. "I'm supposed to be working right now. I'm sure Madam Eva will return soon and will be cross if she thinks I'm distracting you."

"You? A distraction? I hope so." Devlin chuckled, leaning more against her. His eyes drew her.

"Me?" Rebecca questioned. "But I'm not your kind of woman."

"What kind of woman is that?"

"They say you like only fashion models, royals, and debutantes."

"Am I really that shallow?"

Rebecca shrugged.

Is this real? How many times have I dreamt this? But not just like this. Please, if this is a dream, I don't want to wake yet.

He stroked her long, platinum hair and brushed it aside. His fingers outlined her ear, then caressed the suckle scar on her neck. He pressed her body against the settee. She was caught by his dark, bottomless eyes. Devlin sighed and she felt his breath on her skin as she opened her neck for him. Leaning back as he advanced, she longed for his touch. Her head on the back of the sofa but turned, she waited for the pinch when she felt his soft lips graze her scar.

"With just a small bit of venom," he said against her neck. "I could make you very willing. But I'd be like that boyfriend if I did. Part of me wants to take unfair advantage of a fine young woman."

"How do you know I'm a fine young woman?" she asked, a devilish desire filling her thoughts as a coy smile appeared on her lips. "How do you know I'm not willing? You found me in a bar with a violent man."

Devlin's eyes met hers, then her lips with his. Everything inside of her tingled with arousal. She parted her lips, and his tongue found the gap, invading, exploring, and pressing his limits. His arms closed in around her sides and her hands slid up his sleeves. He paused in their embrace as he smiled and observed her from above.

Looking into his eyes again, the same desire that moved her to dance with him the first time so long ago stirred her; as if time hadn't passed. Wanting him even more now than before, she felt his pelvis press against her. With her free hands, she caressed his erection between them. Boldness empowered her desires to be his and overwhelmed propriety.

Devlin appeared surprised, leaning heavier against the back of the settee and her. His breath escaped with a quiver, and she liked the power she held over this stronger-than-human male.

Devlin's face neared hers, then passed her cheek. She presented her neck, accepting if he wanted to suckle. But his lips kissed at her scar and nibbled on her earlobe, careful not to pierce her skin. The contact was intoxicating, and she let out an audible moan that startled her.

"I want you," he whispered, then his lips touched the skin on her neck, and every part of her cried for more. "I've wanted you from the first moment I saw you. But I dared not hope until you took my hand—then the kiss last night."

Her legs and arms felt weak, her stomach filled with

butterflies, and her mind dizzied. His eyes danced over her face, and Rebecca knew that he accepted her without the zombie-like state the venom produced. Their lips touched lightly, then more.

Chapter 9

Desire

Devlin moved over her more, his hand on her neck as the pocket door scraped in the track, and the moment of intense intimacy vaporized. Eva stood in the gap between the two doors. Rebecca slid down the sofa, more under Devlin than before, but knew her long hair would be visible. She imagined the shocked look on Eva's face.

"Oh, my apologies, Lord Devlin," Eva said. "Are you done with my new housekeeper?"

Rebecca assumed Eva saw her hair on the settee and knew what was happening. She squeezed her eyes shut in fear, waiting for Eva's intrusion. She watched Devlin's expression change.

"Apparently not," Devlin growled and flared his fangs, glaring at Eva. "I don't want to be disturbed."

Devlin's fingers extended with long, hard nails like talons as his voice grew gruff. But Rebecca caught his smile as he winked at her.

"And I plan to suckle on her for a while," Devlin ordered harshly. "So, make do without her. She's volunteered herself to me, so no repercussion to her will come of this."

"No, sir," Eva replied humbly.

Rebecca heard the pocket doors scrape as they closed.

Beet red, Rebecca cringed at the thought of another lecture about knowing her place that would come from Eva. They had been caught like two teenagers in the back of a Buick. Devlin was a lord, and she, a mere servant. But she wanted him more with every moment they spent together. Now that she caught his eye, she determined to risk whatever it would take to be with him, even if it was only a moment in time.

Devlin's hands and teeth returned to normal and he repositioned himself so that she was under him again. She appreciated that the interruption hadn't completely took him out of the moment as it did her.

"Privacy is at a premium here," Devlin said, peering down at her.

"I'm sorry," Rebecca said. "I've disgraced you."

"No," he said. "You haven't done anything wrong. Come with me. Perhaps we can find a place to continue this undisturbed?"

Rebecca nodded.

Devlin stood and offered his hand. After she took it, he pulled her abruptly from the sofa against his body. His arms wrapped around her, causing waves of arousal throughout her body, especially as his hands grabbed her ass, forcing her pelvis against his. His lips grazed hers, then they kissed. It was everything she expected and more.

When they parted, he took up one of her hands, lifted it to his face, and kissed it. His eyes flashed, and she felt a nervous anticipation. Like the gentleman he was, he released her, wrapped her hand and arm around his, escorting her to the back hall. Two floors down the soft, plush carpeted stairs, they descended to a room with sandstone walls lighted by sconces. The room housed the stone sarcophagus in the middle; the pre-room before the dungeon.

"Why does your kind have these?" Rebecca asked.

"My kind?" Devlin questioned. Not letting go of her hand, he pulled her close to him and the coffin. "It's just *my kind's* thing."

"I mean," she asked. "Do you really sleep in that?"

"No," Devlin said with a glance at her from beneath his brows. "I hardly sleep at all." He moved to the head of it. "If you're that interested, I'll show you."

He pushed back the lid, which Rebecca could tell was of great weight: over an inch and a half thick, by eight feet, by three feet wide. The lid had a lattice with a creeping rose-carved in it and cold to the touch. It hardly seemed worn, but she knew it was old.

Devlin pushed the lid back to expose most of the sarcophagus. He tried reaching for something, then, reluctantly, climbed in, positioning himself inside. Rebecca waited but, out of curiosity, climbed onto the cover to peer down at him.

"What is this?" he said, then pulled out a book from the shadows. "What do you know, the last place you look, and there it is."

He began to sit up. Rebecca straddled the opening of the sarcophagus, resting her bottom over the carved design on the upper part of the lid. She noticed the dark soil under Devlin's body. The earth he lay in smelled almost wholesome, clean, or maybe fresh, but different than anything she encountered before.

"I like to read down here," Devlin said. "The rest of the house sometimes is too warm for me. And the staff leaves me alone when I come down here."

"It's quiet." Rebecca smiled down at him. "Peaceful, maybe even – lonely?"

He furrowed his brows at her, as if curious.

Then, she knelt over him, untying his pajama bottoms, and pulled them open. Using only her sense of touch with her eyes glued on his face, she exposed him.

"I was going to suggest…." Devlin began. He pointed to one of the walls, but Rebecca ignored him while sliding off the lid and over him.

Her lips found his and they kissed for a while as she felt his erection return. Pulling her skirt and shifting her underwear to the side, she gently lowered herself as he entered her. Surprisingly, his cold engorged penis titillated her. He groaned with every inch of her descent. His eyes rolled back in his head, a smile lifting at the edges of his lips as Rebecca enjoyed pleasing him. Her knees pressed against the sarcophagus' walls and made contact with the soft soil on either side of his hips.

Once she felt filled inside with his erection, she pressed her weight forward, grinding on him. Small gestures afforded considerable friction. Back and forth, angling the head of his penis so it moved in and out of her at the most sensitive area. Bracing her arms against his chest, she rode him and increased her speed.

I know he may think me promiscuous, but it's been too long, and this feels too good to stop.

Devlin reached up, removing the pins from her hair. His hands fell over her front, and she didn't care that he opened her blouse or ran his hands over her bra. He caressed her breasts, her stomach, and eventually, pulled her skirt away to feel her clit.

"My angel, so innocent looking." Devlin pulled her to his lips. "Yet, you are just as impetuous as me."

Rebecca couldn't stop it when her body passed over into its orgasm. Whipping her hair back, she clutched the sides of the coffin, groaning uncontrollably, like several decades of pent-up passion exploding from within. The sensation peaked, and slowly, her groans subsided.

Once done, she looked down at Devlin, who watched her every move and nodded. He played with the platinum locks that grazed his chest.

"It's been such a long time since…" Devlin said. "I've forgotten how good this feels."

Devlin sat up, grabbed her head in his hands and kissed her passionately. Then grasped her hips, moving her, forcing her to continue. He exhaled a loud groan that reverberated off the bare walls, and the acoustics caught her off guard. She felt the throbbing from within her. His chest jerked upward, and his head fell back as his hands squeezed her thighs harder than she expected but she knew he had climaxed. His grip hurt, but only for a second. His hands left her body and grasped the edges of the sarcophagus. It happened a few times before he fell back into the dirt, panting. Rebecca smiled proudly having been the source of his pleasure.

With a fatigued sigh, Devlin glowed. Tired, she pulled her legs from the dirt, resting on the lid again. Buttoning her blouse, she felt Devlin's cold hand brush off the soil from her legs. He sat up and twisted as Rebecca brushed the dirt off his back and out of his hair.

"Thank you," he said, then shook his head with a chuckle.

"What?" she asked.

"I didn't expect this," he said. "Not from you. You were so timid a few days ago."

Devlin climbed to his feet, brushed himself off, and adjusted his pants. Once his feet were on the stone pad that encircled the sarcophagus, he reached for Rebecca and lifted her off. She rearranged her skirt as he brushed more dirt from her legs.

"That was definitely a first." He laughed.

I made him laugh, and this was his first time? No.

"Can't say I ever remember doing it in there," he muttered.

That's what he meant.

Devlin wrapped her arm around his to lead her from the tomb, but her sluggish legs hesitated, and her foot landed on the edge of the marble pad, and she lost her balance. Stumbled slightly, she caught herself before she fell.

"Are you alright?" Devlin asked.

"I feel a bit light-headed and very relaxed," she said. "Almost like I've been drugged."

"I have that effect on women, but here. Come this way."

He helped her to what looked like a wall, but at waist height, there were two handles.

"Lean on me," he said as he took each handle.

With little effort on his part, he opened a different pair of sandstone pocket doors she had mistaken for a wall. They crackled and snapped as they moved apart. He quickly grabbed Rebecca around her waist and pulled her into his arms, carrying her over the threshold.

Unlike the dungeon, this room had been decorated in pastel colors. Drapes covered the stone walls with a round bed in the center covered in silks and satins. The same style sconces lit the space, creating a soft glow. The padded headboard, like the walls, matched the comforter.

Devlin laid her gently on the bed, then removed her shoes. She enjoyed feeling his cold hands as they grazed her skin. He stretched himself behind her and covered them both.

"This is more what I had in mind," he said, snuggling behind her. "Stay here this afternoon. Tonight, I have a thing…"

"*A thing?*" she repeated. His fingers interlocked in hers and rested on her thigh as they spooned.

"I have to attend a *thing* for business. Would you accompany me as—an escort?"

"If you want me to."

"Yes, very much."

"Yes, I'd love to. What kind of an affair is it?"

"It's just a coat and tie thing," Devlin said. "I'll wake you in a few hours."

She felt him behind her, then sleep darkened the room, and she was out.

by K.A. Monaco

Chapter 10

The Thing

Rebecca waited by the Rolls for Devlin, who had forgotten something in his room. It was another pleasant evening in July around six o'clock. Carmichael stood waiting by the car door. She knew he had checked her out when she first arrived. Elizabeth's black, sequined cocktail dress was a little loose, but with the help of a few safety pins, it fit like a glove. And it had been ages since she wore the dark hose with the seam up the back attached to the black garter belt. In the mirror, it made her legs look even longer.

"Damn, you clean up good, Becca," Carmichael said. This time, he was leering. "Smell good, too."

She ignored him, but his ogling felt nice.

Carmichael was very handsome. His dark hair pulled back in a long ponytail with soft brown eyes, and a pleasing smile. He had dated most of the women in the manor over the years except her. Her quiet manners and bookworm habits didn't draw his attention.

I bet he takes notice now. I need to buy one of these dresses for myself. I forgot how it feels to be attractive.

"Sorry." Devlin appeared at the door in a different suit, this one from Versace, in navy blue with a baby blue button-down shirt and a purple tie, which was pulled open for a more casual look. He stroked the long bangs back over his head as he descended the stairs of the manor.

Rebecca smiled as Devlin motioned for her to enter before him. Then he followed, and Carmichael closed the door behind them. She knew Carmichael would still be watching, though he turned all professional.

"You look spot on," Devlin said.

"What?" Rebecca asked, her eyes wide with fear. "I have a spot on this dress? Oh, Elizabeth will kill me if I ruin her dress."

"No, I meant you look perfect for tonight," Devlin explained. "A slang term, it means you look appropriate. But you look better than that. You're beautiful. You really don't get out much, do you?"

"No." Rebecca felt embarrassed when she caught his eyes; they looked hungry and mischievous. Devlin slid closer.

"You look very handsome," she said. "These are Gretta's shoes."

"Why don't you have your own clothes?"

"I don't go out enough to justify it," she replied.

"Yeah," Carmichael said from the front seat. Devlin seemed captured, looking into her eyes while Carmichael continued. "Something always happens when she leaves the house, right, Becca? Like a few years ago – those two guys started fighting over you, and it ended up in a huge pub brawl. God, that was fun."

"Thank you, Carmichael," Devlin said, reaching over

Rebecca to raise the window that separated the front and back seats. Once up, his focus unchanged, she felt a thrill run up her spine yet timid, and nervous butterflies in her stomach.

"I guess, I'm just a home body," she said.

"Nothing wrong with that." He grazed her face with his cold fingers.

"But Madam has organized trips to the zoo and the gardens," she stammered on nervously. "And once we went to the opera."

"Did you like it? The opera?" he asked.

"Margaret had to interpret, since she came from Italy during the 1879 European migration. But, yes, I loved it."

"Good." Devlin drew closer. She swallowed hard and felt arousal between her legs. "I'd like to take you, sometime."

He kissed her gently, lingering and the feeling of his lips against hers was like silk. Her hands instinctively touched his face and pulled him to her. Almost losing his balance, his hand fell to her thigh as he leaned in, then tightened at her leg, his thumb close to her women parts. She stiffened, inhaled, and smiled.

"A garter belt?" he asked with a coy smile.

"I don't like panty hose," she replied. "Why? Don't you like garter belts?"

"I love vintage lingerie and all that forties apparel."

"It was new in my day. I guess I'm old fashioned."

"I like old fashioned." He kissed her harder, passionately, as the city blocks passed outside their window, unobserved.

A knock on the divider alerted them that they were about to

arrive. Devlin adjusted his jacket as Rebecca took his handkerchief from his jacket pocket and wiped the lipstick from his face.

"Thank you." He looked out the window on her side. "Now, about tonight, mingle but don't talk much. These people will think of you as just an escort, but some may try to find out things about me through you. You don't work for me."

"I understand." Rebecca turned to the window to see the venue as the car slowed. "I'm just the dame of the week on your arm, a symbol of your ability to conquer, a sign that you're heterosexual, and a good excuse to depart a boring conversation or the event early. You'll leave everyone with the impression we have some other party or event that is more important—or intimate to go to."

"Exactly." Devlin smirked. "You catch on quick."

"I got around in my former days. Social circles must not have changed much."

"No, not really."

***

The party was glamorous and well-attended. Most men wore black tuxedos, and the women wore evening gowns. Devlin was oblivious that he was underdressed. No one else noticed or made a comment. He held Rebecca's hand while they mingled, greeted, and introduced her to so many different people that she knew she would never remember their names. But she didn't care; most likely, she'd never meet these people again. After hiding in the manor for so long, she felt important in this momentary spotlight while hanging on Devlin's arm.

"I'll get us something to drink, alright?" Rebecca asked as she quietly waited by Devlin's side.

They had their own little audience of men dressed in black tuxedos and their bored spouses. Devlin was focused on the conversation, but nodded and squeezed her hand slightly before she abandoned him. Heading for the bar, four women from the group split off and followed her. Each tried to compliment her on her figure, dress, or hair. She stood amongst them quietly as each tried their best to over-talk the others.

"And Albert's place is the best. If you have never gone, call me and I'll introduce you," one of the women said.

"Thank you," Rebecca replied. "I don't need a personal hairdresser."

At the crowded bar, she waited for the bartender while the women chatter around her. She ignored them to get the bartender's attention.

"Bloody Mary and a brandy, two fingers high, please?" Rebecca asked.

The bartender nodded, and soon, two glasses appeared before her. The one drew her attention and she found herself salivating before placing the tall glass to her lips. She sipped in the saucy red liquid but it surprised her. It didn't taste like what she thought it should.

"Are you sure this is a Bloody Mary?" she asked the bartender.

"By the book," he said, then disappeared.

Rebecca shrugged to herself, thinking it was the vodka brand that made the difference. She turned to locate Devlin again when a man approached and prominently stood before her. Taking the glasses from her hands, he placed them on the bar.

"Dance with me," the man said.

He was older, handsome with gray at his temples, and a strong self-confidence. The man took her hand, but she remained unmoved. His boldness lacked any charm.

"A gentleman doesn't demand, he asks," Rebecca replied. "I don't wish to dance with you."

"That's right," Rebecca heard Devlin's voice behind her. "Find another."

The man grimaced, then melted into the crowd as Rebecca turned and shined a relieved smile in Devlin's direction. She picked up the glasses and handed him one.

"You could have danced," Devlin said. "I wouldn't mind."

"I want to be like lady luck, tonight." Rebecca took his hand. "I'll stay with the man I came with."

"I like that." Devlin leaned closer to her ear. "I like you. I like your loyalty. But you do know that every man here whose heads you have turned at least once will make love to their wives tonight with you in their fantasies."

She leaned to his ear. "I don't care what they do, as long as tonight I'm in *your* fantasies."

Devlin squeezed her hand. His eyes danced, and he inhaled, excited. "Does that mean I might have another taste—like this afternoon?"

"I don't know, we'll see." She returned a devious glance.

A chime sounded, and the crowd hushed. Another, and like cattle, the group moved toward the double doors in the rear of the room. Rebecca could see beyond the crowd to a banquet hall.

"Fire alarm?" she asked.

"No, wish it was," Devlin said, catching her eye with a smirk. "It means the monkey does his dance."

"What does that mean?"

"You'll see."

He placed his drink on a passing tray, then grabbed her hand. They moved with the crowd to the banquet room. But before she entered, she noticed an easel with a picture of Devlin on the front with the letters APFA over his name.

"They're throwing this *thing* for you?" Rebecca asked. "What did that sign mean?"

"It means I need to speak before we can go home." He sounded slightly annoyed.

"If this is for you…." Rebecca stopped, tightened her hand holding his, and forced him to turn to face her. "You should have worn your tux—I know you have one, especially if you need to make a speech."

"You *are* old school, aren't you?" Devlin said with a shake of his head and a chuckle. "It makes me look even paler than I already am. Besides, when you've been to as many of these things as I have…"

She buttoned the top of his dress shirt and cinched up his tie with a motherly smirk on her face. Grabbing her hands to stop her, he held them under his chin with a devious smile. She thought he might be annoyed with her hen-pecking, but he looked at her oddly affectionately.

"…you dress for comfort," he continued. "They consider me eccentric. And it works when you're rich. Besides, this is just an excuse for them to eat too much, drink too much, and dress like rich people. Come on. Once I make my appearance, my obligation is *done*."

His smile and how his eyes danced over her face made her believe this was normal or just a pre-requisite to afford him the lifestyle he liked.

"Okay."

The banquet hall quickly filled as the group sat at round tables with white linen tablecloths. Beautiful crystal chandeliers hung from the ceiling. The wine flowed, the goblets were filled, and the food servers cleared the dishes away when she and Devlin arrived. He pushed her before him. Placing one hand on her arm and the other on the small of her back, he navigated her through the room.

Devlin shook a few hands and waved at others while dodging the waiters on his way to the stage. Rebecca realized he was holding her hand not to keep her close but to give others the illusion that he was warmer than room temperature or the cold she had become accustomed to. But she wasn't all that warm either. Ever since the fevers, the circulation in her hands and feet had suffered.

The MC took the microphone to make an announcement. Devlin motioned for her to remain in the shadows. She nodded.

His short speech seemed well rehearsed, almost effortless. He held up the giant cardboard check handed to him, then gave it to someone else. He spoke about how it was his pleasure to be here, of corporate responsibility, and helping the less fortunate. And none of it seemed like the man that took her to the movies the night before. She realized all the pomp and circumstance was a facade for the public. If they really knew him, they wouldn't be honoring him in this fashion, but probably chasing him with pitchforks and torches.

Devlin nodded to the applause as he moved across the stage and descended the stairs to be by her side a second later. Flanked by well-wishers and the line of those to shake his hand, Devlin grabbed her arm.

"Let's see if we can make a mad dash for the door," he said with a coy smile.

"We can stay if you like," Rebecca replied. But a second later, he moved swiftly and she found it hard to keep up with his pace in her heels.

His plan soon failed as others distracted him from his escape. But when a path to the doors cleared, Devlin resumed his gait when the music from the band erupted and caught him like a deer in the headlights. Rebecca recognized the tempo, the whine of the violins, as the band began a tango. Devlin stopped dead in his European shoes, and she bumped into him.

"It would be...." Devlin muttered when he turned to Rebecca. "I can't resist the tango. Can you...? Do you know how to tango?"

Rebecca nodded. "But it's been a while."

"How stupid of me. Where are my manners?" Devlin held out his hand. "Would you do me the honor of this dance?"

"Yes, thank you."

Taking his hand, he turned her into his arms. Cheek to cheek, they joined the two other couples on the dance floor. The other dancers didn't draw the attention that Devlin did, and soon, a crowd watched from the sides. Rebecca tried not to notice for fear she would make a mistake.

Devlin led her well, and she read his body language like they had danced together for years. His hands slid down her sides. Appearing effortless, Rebecca caved into his body as he moved her around the floor. Seductively, she slid down his legs, her hands wrapped around his thighs when he grabbed her under the arms and lifted her to her feet just as the music ended.

On the last beat, he leaned her backward in a dip just above the floor; with one hand under her backside and the other on the outer side of her bent knee that rested against his hip. She had forgotten the exhilaration of dancing. Upside down, it was the first time she took a long look at the crowd as she panted.

So many people watching. I wonder if this dress is keeping my cleavage in?

Devlin's strong arms pulled her to his chest, still in the dip, her arms wrapped around his shoulder, and their eyes met. She could see by the recognition in his eyes that she was no longer Becca the simple maid. She felt panicked.

"Rebecca? Bloody hell, you're alive?" he whispered, his voice broke. "We danced the tango before. Like your story, your boyfriend shot you. But your hair color was dark and your eyes were light blue like the sky—Roberts said you died."

Devlin's face clouded; his brow furrowed. With so many on-lookers, this conversation needed to be in private. She had hoped he'd forgotten about that girl she used to be. But apparently, he never forgot her which both relieved her fears and horrified her.

"I—go by Becca now," she stuttered as Devlin brought her back to her feet. Looking into his eyes, the crowd lessened in priority.

"Why didn't they tell me you lived?" Devlin asked, his voice a choked whisper. His eyes glared under his brow yet seemed as to become misty.

"Because I asked Madam Eva not to." Rebecca tried to step away perceiving the many eyes still upon them, but he held her tight against him. She felt the world closing in around them.

"Why?" he demanded.

"I can explain, but do you really want to do it here?" she asked as his grip tightened. "Can we please leave?"

"Of course," Devlin growled.

Releasing her, he gestured like a gentleman for her to go before him. Sorrow filled her heart for the way he looked at her. She headed for the double doors when his cold hand clasped around her fore arm and aggressively led her out of the banquet hall. An attempt to stop him by another couple received his less than cordial regard as he pulled her along hastily.

Rebecca looked forward to the night air as old memories surfaced. In flashes, she remembered Tony, the sharp smack to her face, and the hot, burning metal from the bullet.

Down the crowded elevator, several halls, and out the front, Devlin remained silent. Carmichael leaned against the hood of the Rolls waiting for them. Devlin dove in the back first, and Rebecca followed reluctantly while Carmichael held the door and shut it behind her. When she entered, Devlin sat on the opposite side of the bench seat, staring out the window. His fingers pressed his lips, and she perceived his anger.

Everything was going so well. Why did he have to remember me now?

"Home, sir?" Carmichael asked once he sat in the driver's seat.

"No, I want to go to my happy place," Devlin growled.

"Yes, sir," Carmichael replied.

"*Happy place?*" Rebecca asked sheepishly.

"You'll see." Devlin snapped. "We need to talk, but not here—or at home."

Rebecca nodded. She felt a lump in her throat as memories of her past life drifted around her mind. This moment she had avoided for decades.

How is it possible I still love him. But what if he's so angry

by K.A. Monaco

that he doesn't want me?

Chapter 11

Happy Place

The high full moon and its reflection on the Hudson River enchanted Rebecca. In the distance, she saw the city lights of New York and knew they stood on the New Jersey side. Carmichael placed a bottle of wine and a blanket on the park bench, then he vanished back into the driver's seat of the car that waited yards away at the curb. The sound of the waves lapped at the rocks between the path and the deep. The breeze from the water made the night in July feel more like March. A long cobblestone path led to the waterfront.

Devlin walked from the car with his hands in his pockets and his head low. He stood at the water's edge where the cobblestone ended with his back to her. Rebecca sat on one of the park benches and opened the bottle of wine. She took a deep breath of the fresh air as her eyes searched the horizon at all the beautiful lights, but his silence hurt more than she thought it would.

She walked to his side. Though he appeared calm, he still clenched his teeth and avoided looking at her. Afraid to speak, she knew this situation had been hers to own. She had delayed too long in facing him, and for that, she felt sorry.

"You call this your happy place?" Rebecca asked, breaking the silence.

"Yes," Devlin replied. "At night, it's quiet and deserted. Something about the water is always calming to me."

"What time is it?"

"Ten, I think." Devlin continued to look out at the black, glassy waters.

"It doesn't feel like ten o'clock." A momentary quiet, and the small talk felt empty.

"Why didn't you tell me?" Devlin asked, kicking the pebbles at his feet. "You were right under my nose all those years. You don't know how I longed for you. Why?"

He turned, looking down at her, yet she didn't see anger in his eyes, only pain.

"I was afraid," Rebecca said, but those fears seemed shallow and powerless. She realized she used them as excuses to avoid this moment.

"Afraid of what?"

"Afraid you wouldn't want me. Afraid I'd never be enough for you. You know the wounds I sustained left me unable to have children. I woke in a hospital after several months in a coma with a skull fracture and multiple broken bones. They said I had been tossed out of a Duesenberg automobile like a sack of potatoes. And yet I have no memory of it. When I left there, I wandered back to my old neighborhood, but my family were gone. My father killed himself, my mother couldn't make ends meet when I vanished, and she left. I had no place to go. I remember waking under a bush in Central Park with this horrible lost feeling. In fact, most mornings I awake with that feeling still."

Rebecca wiped her eyes.

"Then I wandered aimlessly until I stood in front of the Manor. I have no idea how I got there. Madam Eva recognized me; I don't know how because I didn't even recognize myself. I looked like two steps from the grave. She wanted to tell you, but I asked her not to because I didn't want you to see me that way. I remained that way for years. After consulting several doctors, one suggested tomato juice, and that seemed to help. But ever since—I've never felt whole or complete. I still wake in cold sweats and panic, wondering where I am. I can't remember everything. How could I offer myself to you if I still don't feel right inside with myself?"

Rebecca paused. Devlin waited silently.

"Months turned to years, then to decades, and those things haven't changed. I remember who I used to be, so beautiful I could stop traffic. My face got me out of some major jams. And you didn't meet me in a speakeasy by accident. It was the place to be. I dated a gangster. And I knew that at any moment a rivel gang could find that place and blow us all away. But it made me feel alive. I was surrounded by dangerous men and I was young. I felt bullet proof, as ironic as that is.

"I lost the hope that we would mean anything to each other. I hid from you, and I'm sorry. Please don't hold it against Eva for not telling you because I asked her not to. After the fevers and the broken bones, I feared life. I hid in the kitchen afraid of my own shadow. I was a shell of a being. I began to read about characters and knew I was like them, once. But no more. I escaped my fears that way.

"After being shot, I've developed an intense reaction to wounds and blood. You see, I'm nothing like the woman you met that night. She was fearless while I'm fearful. You deserved better than what I've become.

"I told myself you were happy and better off without me. That the affection you developed for me stemmed from some misguided Nightingale Syndrome. How could you want me now? Just because you saved me, didn't mean you wanted me to be a burden on you. Roberts made it very clear I was a drain on you and the staff."

"Roberts didn't speak for me," Devlin said.

"Why did you save me?" she asked.

She felt as if he had peered down into her soul and saw how insufficient she was in her own eyes.

"I admired you for your bravery," Devlin said. "You wanted to save me. Do you know how rare that is? For most of my life, your people have wanted to kill me. Granted, you didn't know what I am. But I didn't want you to die and I felt responsible for what happened to you because I interfered in your life. Had I not come along, you might have had children, raised a family, died of old age…"

"Or been beaten to death by my boyfriend," Rebecca said. "You don't know what would have happened."

"And I thought I fell in love with you," Devlin said. "At least I wanted to have that chance to see if it would last. I never felt anything so strong."

"I felt it, too. But part of me has been afraid you would assume I'm still that spontaneous, free-spirited girl. The longer time marched on, the more insignificant I felt. It's grown harder each year to even think of speaking to you. Time has a way of doing that."

"I know that," Devlin sighed. "You don't think I'm afraid, too?"

"You're not human like me. What do you have to be afraid of?"

"It still hurts to be rejected. No matter how old you are. As you can tell, I didn't develop a supernatural confidence with my other abilities. I'm still me on the inside, older but not wiser. I never believed in love at first sight—until you."

"Is that why you never married again?" Rebecca asked.

"I entertained the thoughts, but every time I try, I found myself comparing them to you."

"You could have anyone you want," Rebecca said. "Why would you want someone as flawed as me?"

"I don't see flaws, I see beauty. You're so young." He touched her cheek. "Sweet, uncomplicated, and welcoming. So, what was this afternoon, if not spontaneous?"

"I don't know," she replied. "Decades of desire, longing and loneliness. Loving you from the shadows. With my life a never-ending fear-fest … you gave me peace. But I couldn't jeopardize that while I felt so weak and frail. Knowing you desired me once was the only solace I had. And you never changed. But I couldn't risk your rejection. I'm prettier than I've been in a long time and I gained a little of my confidence back. When you took notice to me, I couldn't help myself. I had to feel your touch again."

The sound of the water lapping on the rocks a few yards away distracted her. She didn't want to let her desires run away with her. And if he continued talking so intimately, she'd surely lose herself in hope.

"Do you hate me for not telling you?" she asked timidly.

"No," Devlin replied. He pulled her chin up with his fingers, maintaining eye contact. "But I understand. Time has changed us both. It would be wise to take this slow."

Devlin pulled her close and swayed gently. "Dance with me."

"But there's no music," Rebecca replied.

Devlin hummed and held her body against his as she matched his rhythm. At an appropriate bend in the tune, he turned her out, then under his arm to return to his embrace. She tucked in close as her arms found their way beneath his suit coat. They swayed, his arms around her back as she leaned her head against his chest.

"All those months you were ill, first from the wound then the fevers. But this is all I wanted from you. To hold you, to move with you … to love you."

Rebecca stopped and moved to look into his face.

His eyes sparkled under the streetlights. "I don't know if I can take this slow. I don't want to scare you."

"You won't."

Rebecca rose to her tippy toes and their lips met. Their kiss turned passionate. Enveloped in his arms, the world around her faded away. Her dreams never took her this far, but it wouldn't stop her now.

"Get a room," said a man walking by.

Devlin hissed at him, which broke their moment of intimacy. Devlin ran his hand down her arm as she stepped back.

Can't we get any privacy?

"You're cold. I'm sorry I have such little body heat. Come on."

"Since the fevers, I'm always cold. It's not your fault."

"Ah, but I can fix it." He had a contagious smile.

Devlin moved toward the park bench where Carmichael had placed the items. Picking up the blanket, he wrapped her in it. With the warmth, she felt satisfied as she basked in his presence. Her desires becoming reality blew her mind and captivated her thoughts. There would be no future or past, only now. They sat and she handed him a glass of wine, but the lack of conversation made her nervous.

"So, what was that whole dog and pony show for tonight?" she asked.

"APSA," Devlin replied.

"I saw that on the poster; what does it mean?"

"Apex Predator Sustenance Association," Devlin said as he sipped his wine.

"Are you serious?" Rebecca laughed. "And you tell people

that?"

"No, but we don't hide it either." Devlin put his arm around her. "That's the legal name. But when asked, I usually come up with something clever or stupid: Acme Pestilence Subsidiary Association, All Paws Sanctuary for Animals or—my favorite—Association for the Preservation of Silly Acronyms. No one gives a bloody damn when you're throwing large sums of money at their cause. Like that *thing* tonight – it was about human trafficking. The Association is all about the betterment of mankind. We fund the drilling of wells in Africa, the eradication of human slavery and child labor, and even prisoner reform."

"We?" she asked.

"The Association is more or less a front for my uncles and me. It keeps us social. Every twenty years or so, one of us becomes the face of the Association to keep it alive, allowing the other to sink back into anonymity so our ongoing youth doesn't draw attention. This is my twenty-year limelight."

"Does it displease you to be in the public eye?" she asked. She took his hand in hers as they had at the movies. Staring out into the night sky, she could sense him relaxing.

"It's not so bad. Granted, I had the most ruffles and highest-powdered wig back in the day, but now it's more about portfolios and how liquid your assets are."

"I don't claim to understand all that. You and your uncles must be very smart."

"No, we've had a long time to learn how. You know, trial and error."

"Are your uncle's blood-related?"

"If you mean other than our form of nutrition, only Viktor and I are related; the others are – how do they say it now … brother by another mother? My mother was Russian and married my father, who was an English lord. The title doesn't mean much today."

"Where are your parents? Why aren't there more like you around?" Rebecca asked. "I'm sorry, I shouldn't pry."

"No, I don't mind you asking." Devlin sighed. "A long time ago, Uncle Viktor saw how our fellow kind created fear in humans by feeding indiscriminately. It drew attention to our kind, and some in high places didn't want that. Two factions developed. My so-called family and *theirs*. *Theirs* were of greater numbers, but through less than respectable means, my uncles made *them* extinct. My father was one of *them*. My mother said one of my kind did him in."

"I'm sorry," Rebecca said between sips. "Did you miss growing up without a father?"

"No, I had Viktor, and back then, she told me it was an arranged marriage. It wasn't like they loved or even liked each other."

"I thought your kind lived forever."

"Not our women. Something about a woman's reproduction system causes them to be more prone to illness and injury. Now, my real aunt, Olga, was barren before she was turned. She's been with Viktor from the beginning. She's our beta example. We can only conclude it has something to do with her lack of reproduction that has given her longevity."

"When were you turned?"

"You're full of questions tonight." He smiled.

"I'm sorry."

"No, I like this. Not many people take a real interest in me. They think they know me from my face on the cover of a magazine or interview. But I don't have many people who really know me." He pulled her closer, snuggling as he scanned the sky over the bay. "My mother turned me before she died. I was twenty-five. That was such a long time ago, but a day hasn't gone by that I don't think about her. I miss her. Viktor gave her permission to change me. But anyone who is changed now must be approved by all of us to protect our food source."

"Why prisoners, and why bother reforming them?"

"Would you want to eat tainted meat?" Devlin asked.

Rebecca shook her head no.

"We reform them; end their drug habit so that we can partake. But not Viktor. He has friends in high places, so his vessel of choice is political prisoners. Most of them aren't drug addicts, and in his society, political prisoners disappear easily." He winked at her. "And I feel like we're lessening the burden of society by removing some from the penal system."

He's so down-to-earth and genuine. Not all mysterious or cryptic, except for the vampire thing.

"Do you tell all your escorts this stuff?" Rebecca asked, smiling.

"No, but yesterday, at the movies, I don't know. I felt so relaxed with you. Now I know why I do, Rebecca. How I've missed you."

Chapter 12

Again?

Devlin touched her cheek with his ice-cold hands, and it surprised her. He leaned in, and their lips met. Several kisses later, as they could have continued more deeply, Rebecca heard his body grumble and pulled away. The thought of him feeding sobered her.

"I guess we should be going," Devlin said, tossing the wine onto the grass. "I'm hungry."

"And your dinner is waiting at the manor?" she asked.

He nodded.

Rebecca stood as Devlin gathered the wine bottle and blanket.

"You go on ahead," Devlin said. "You must be cold."

Rebecca nodded and started for the Rolls. The wind caught her from behind as her long hair blinded her for only a moment. When she pulled her hair out of her sight, a motorcycle jumped the curb and roared to a stop before her. The driver was a grungy, greasy man with a long, scraggly beard and a baseball cap on backward. He eyed her from head to toe, which made her skin crawl.

"You look like you need someone to show you a good time,"

the biker said. "Get on."

"No, thank you," Rebecca replied, side-stepping the bike to head for the Rolls.

The man grabbed her arm and pulled her closer. Rebecca smelled the liquor on his breath, his repugnant body odor, and the exhaust of the bike. She tried to break away, but he tightened his grip.

"I wasn't asking," he said. "I told you to get on."

"I said no!" Rebecca resisted more, but the biker held fast, and it scared her.

"I'm not leaving here without you." The biker tried to drag her over his lap, but Rebecca fought.

Before she could take another breath of his foul persona, Devlin stood behind him. He dropped the items in his hands, and the wine bottle shattered against the paved walk. With one hand, Devlin lifted the driver off his bike and tossed the man to the ground so hard that she heard a snap of a bone breaking. The man cried out.

Devlin's well-shined black shoe nestled under the biker's beard and against his neck, pinning him to the cobblestone. The bike teetered to one side, then fell with a crash.

"The woman said no." Devlin ground his foot as the biker tried to push it off.

"But she's mine," the biker said, his voice changed as he struggled to breathe. "No one else can possess her but me."

"Go to the car, Rebecca," Devlin ordered.

Rebecca began to back away, then turned for the car.

Carmichael appeared with a tire iron. She felt shaken, and Carmichael held her as he escorted her to the back door of the limo.

"I'm not a man you antagonize," Devlin growled. "And I eat men like you for breakfast."

At the car, Rebecca turned to see Devlin had released his foot but grabbed the biker by the throat before the man could sit up. Devlin tossed him a good distance. The man landed on the cobblestone path further into the park and didn't move.

Carmichael pulled open the car door for her, then retreated to the driver's side.

"This only happens when *you* leave the manor," Carmichael said as he disappeared into the car.

She turned, and Devlin was instantly behind her, holding the car door for her and blocking her view of the man on the ground.

"Are you alright?" Devlin asked. "He didn't hurt you, did he?"

Rebecca trembled when he touched her arm. She climbed in the back, and Devlin followed. As Rebecca rested on the seat, she realized she breathed heavily, her hands shook, and tears dotted her cheeks. Carmichael quickly pulled away from the curb and accelerated with enough force to push her back in the seat.

"You're not alright," Devlin whispered, pulling Rebecca to his chest.

He held her for a while as her fears slowly vanished and she calmed.

"You weren't exaggerating," Devlin said softly. "The crazies do come out of the woodwork when you leave the manor."

"Is she alright, sir?" Carmichael turned back to catch a glimpse. "It's a good thing you were close to her. I don't think I could have handled him alone."

Devlin pushed the button on the window between the sections of the car.

"I told you this happens all..." Carmichael's voice trailed off as the divider sealed.

"Feeling better, love?" Devlin pulled her away slightly. "Odd, you had a man act similar at *the thing* tonight. For a woman who sees herself as vulnerable and insignificant, you certainly have a power over men."

Rebecca nodded but felt agitated. She looked into his eyes, then kissed him. The fear had turned into something she didn't want to repress. Her lips became a wild frenzy. Devlin welcomed her, grabbing the back of her neck with one hand as the other held her side, pulling her in.

After a moment, Devlin pushed her back and down onto the rear seat. His body on top of hers caused her senses to run wild with arousal.

"Chivalry turns me on, apparently," she muttered, kissing his lips as her hands framed his face.

"Do you reward all those who rescue you like this?"

"No, just you." They resumed passionate kissing.

The car arrived home as they were wrapped in each other's embrace, but they didn't stop for a while. Carmichael was long gone when Devlin pulled away and his stomach growled again. Leaving the car, he led her down the back stairs into the basement, but when faced with going to the dungeon, Rebecca hesitated. She wanted to be with him more than anything, but the thought of that room made her stomach twinge and groan.

"Forgive me," Devlin said. "I forgot how the sight and smell of blood makes you ill."

"I don't mean to be disrespectful," Rebecca said. "But I can't..."

"Not at all, love." Devlin glowed. "But I don't want the evening to end."

"Neither do I," she replied.

His smile seemed wider than she remembered. He pressed her against the pocket doors that led to the room they had napped in and kissed her hard. His arousal was apparent, and she could have encouraged him, but she knew he needed to eat.

"We're very much alike, you and I," he said. "We both like books and meals at home."

"Eating out is overrated," she smirked.

"Rest while I—am detained."

Devlin opened the pocket doors to the bedroom. She stepped in when he grabbed her again, kissing her passionately. He left no doubt in her mind about his expectations for later.

"I'll be back soon," he said, backing away and closing the doors.

Undressing, she slipped beneath the silken blankets. This was not the ceremony of the 'Crumbs' which took place the day he arrived. This time he ate alone with only Carmichael's assistance.

The desire to sleep surprised her, having odd slumber habits and being aroused. Most nights, she usually could not fall asleep before early morning. And even then, an hour or two was enough. She slept sounder than she ever could remember.

Only in a light twilight of sleep, the sound of the stone pocket doors crackled as they opened. Then closed. She lay still, aware of the commotion behind her. The blankets moved, and she felt an influx of cool air against her back and legs. The bed jostled, and she felt something cold against her backside. Devlin spooned her from behind. She touched his arm, and before he could move it, she pulled it around her, tucking it against her bare chest.

"You're so warm and soft," Devlin whispered.

"Too warm," she replied. "You feel good."

On her neck, she felt his lips softly, slowly kiss. Each small touch aroused her more.

"You've made me so happy," Devlin said. "I'd like to bite you if I didn't have fangs."

"I guess a little bite wouldn't hurt," she lied, only wanting to please him.

"No, I want you just as you are," he said and snuggled tight. "I want to make love to you in *my own* way."

"This is all I ever wanted."

"That's hard for me to believe."

She moved, and he released her to turn to face him. She

glared at him, confused.

"Only my first two wives I could believe that of," he said. "But even they didn't make me feel like you do. What you and I did in the sarcophagus was lovely, and a first for me. Never have any of my wives ever accompanied me on such an erotic romp in my coffin before. But I prefer to make love to you in soft sheets and a firm mattress."

Devlin changed positions, laying over her with his elbows under her shoulders as he pressed her against the bed. He held her head in his hands. Rebecca cupped his jaw, kissing him gently all over his face and neck. He kissed her back, and as the passion mounted. Rebecca slid her knees up until her inner thighs were along his outer thighs. She felt the pressure as he pressed his erection into her, and instantly, the pleasure was more than before. Her head tilted back with her chin to the ceiling, letting out a moan. Non-stop, Devlin continued to caress and kiss her skin with his soft lips. One of his hands cupped her breast, then moved to her leg. His cold hands refreshed and aroused her. Her feet found the back of his calves and moved along his legs.

He seemed harder than before. Pleased he wanted her again, Rebecca gave into him, holding onto his neck as the pleasure mounted with every thrust. For minutes or hours, she didn't care. It felt better than what she remembered of sex. She wanted him more as she approached her first orgasm, thinking he would end quickly after hers.

They moaned in sync with his rhythmic thrusts as he

continued to roll her around in the bed in different positions. Then, surprised, she orgasmed a second time, but he still didn't climax. She felt like putty in his hands and was willing to give him anything he wanted.

Finally, he maneuvered her into a position she had seen in a Kama Sutra book in his library. She arched her back, wrapped her hand around his neck while seated in his lap. He caressed her breasts, sucking on her nipples that almost brought her to her third orgasm. But Devlin pulled her to face him, and to Rebecca, he seemed to enjoy kissing her lips more. He moved her only enough that when she erupted the last time, she shrieked in surprise.

Then one arm wrapped around her waist for the final throws, Devlin used his strength to lift her up and down his shaft. When he stopped, he squeezed her tight as his pleasure manifested in groans exploded out of him. She could feel his erection within her throbbing as he climaxed. He swallowed hard, and his chest quivered until it was over.

Devlin hesitated to leave the moment as their afterglow persisted. He brushed her long hair away from her shoulder, leaning her back onto the pillow and kissing her tenderly.

"It's been a very long time since anyone has offered…" Devlin paused. "I mean to say thank you."

"My pleasure, my lord."

"Please, love," he begged. "Don't lower yourself to me, not right now."

He fell to her side, pulled her to his chest, and caressed her back as her face lay against his breast. She realized there was the absence of a constant heartbeat, and his abdomen gurgled, which she assumed to be digestion. It slightly disgusted her thinking of what he had eaten.

"How many wives have you had?" Rebecca asked.

"I remember their faces better than their names. Too many," he replied.

Rebecca didn't like the absence of warmth or the stillness in his chest. She re-arranged herself until his arm was under her neck, and they both stared at the ceiling.

"Madam says the others like you have only had a few wives. Is that true?"

"My uncles? Yes." Devlin stroked her hair. "Viktor is still on his first wife. Hans, he's had three. Miguel's on his second and Phillip's at ten, I believe."

"Ten?"

"Yeah, but I'm considered the playboy in the family. A true philanderer compared to the others. I think I've been married eighteen, maybe nineteen times."

"Why haven't you married again?"

"It hurts too much every time it ends. I love too deeply and don't always pick the right women. They marry me for my money, my lands, or sex, but never for me. It's not easy to find a soul mate. Sometimes, it just comes down to not being alone."

"How old are you?" she asked. "If you don't mind me asking."

"Over five hundred," Devlin replied. "Why? Do you want to buy me a birthday present? Because I don't celebrate them anymore. Too depressing."

"Why do you need to be so rich?"

"Well, we needed to be wealthy to do what we want. So, over the years, we took over the banking systems in key countries. We don't flaunt it. Viktor is part of the oligarchy but keeps a low profile, even with them. I'm not what the world thinks of my kind. I've seen the rise and fall of many nations. I care about what happens. I'm always the first to enlist for battle, not just because of my feeding habits. When war ends, I relieve the penal system of its bad eggs. I pay my taxes, vote, and pledge my allegiance to whatever country I live in. I have no desire to rule the world. I'm just happy to be part of it. You find me strange, don't you?"

"No, I admire you. So, you don't meet the world's criteria for your kind. I don't think of you as evil. Not as the world would."

"They would think of me as a monster." Devlin leaned over her, kissing her lips. She played with his hair and snuggled in the warm sheets. Slowly, his body warmed against hers.

"You leave tomorrow, don't you?" Rebecca asked.

"Yes," he replied. But she could hear dissatisfaction in his voice.

For an hour or more, they laughed, chatted, and played with each other, caressing and enjoying their intimacy. Rebecca found him an extremely gentle and fun lover. He tickled her and worshiped her body, making comments that no man had ever said to her. Since the surgery, she felt insecure about others seeing her abdominal scar. But he knew more about it than anyone and she didn't have to explain. He kissed it gently. And she cherished every moment.

If time had not parted us, would it still have been like this?

Surrounded by the stone walls, time stood still. Rebecca didn't know if it was day or night, rainy or sunny, and didn't care. She had lived in this house for almost eighty-five years, and each day seemed the same as the last, but not now. This week stood out like no other. Even if it never happened again, she wouldn't regret it. She knew her place in the household, and to expect that to change was foolish. This was a brief romp with forbidden fruit. The banter trailed off, and Rebecca slipped into slumber.

Chapter 13

Expectations

As she slowly awoke, the room lay still and cold. The bed beside her empty, and the pocket doors left wide open. After a time, she made the bed and scaled the stairs to find the house as always, with servants doing their chores. She slinked up to her little room, showered, and dressed. She held the black, sequined cocktail dress to her face, inhaling the scent of his cologne before placing it back in Elizabeth's closet.

Rebecca adjusted her mindset to return to her humble status and descended to her place in the household, both socially and emotionally. Despite Lord Devlin's orders, she knew there would be no escape without some jab or condescending tongue-lashing from the head housekeeper. She didn't resent being a servant, and to expect that to change was foolish.

Rebecca entered the kitchen, looking forward to something to eat. She wondered what the refrigerator held that would squelch the nagging in her stomach. Several of the staff sat at the long oak table with bench seats. Spying the fridge, she salivated for the daily tomato juice she drank.

"How could you?" Eva demanded.

Eva sat with her back to the door, sipping from a white porcelain cup. All the other servants evacuated, and Rebecca knew the repercussions were about to commence. She stopped short of the table, just behind Eva's right shoulder. Eva set the cup of tea down and stood to address her. Eva's scowling, downward face wrinkled more as she rose to her full height, resembling an older, spiteful woman Rebecca knew before coming to the manor.

"What has taken place between Lord Devlin and me is none of your business," Rebecca said boldly.

"For the last few decades, we have enjoyed a peaceful existence without the torment of one of the master's wives," Eva said. "Now that you've brought back his libido, there'll be a parade of women here, in London, and Stockholm, who will plague our existence at least until he chooses one. And whether he chooses to create one or entertain one of *our kind* – we'll be subject to their spoiled, underhanded, lying ways. They'll disrespect us, spend the lord's money like a never-ending stream, and in the end, he'll kill her for either her lack of loyalty or discretion. In which case, the parade will begin again."

"Why didn't you tell him who I was, that I was alive?" Rebecca asked.

"You asked me not to. Besides, you lived here. You had every chance and chose not to. Why should I play cupid for you? You're an employee, nothing more, nothing less. You should have left well enough alone. And don't think you'll get preferential treatment after this."

"I'm not looking to be treated any differently. I only wanted to make him happy, and I did."

Eva scoffed. "He has money and freedom; he goes where he likes and does what he wants. He's happy enough."

"No, he's not because he has no one to share it with. He's lonely."

"So am I. Don't you think we all would love to feel a connection, to be part of someone else? But you can't trust anyone with our secrets unless they work here."

"You always discourage me from that; why do you treat me differently?"

"Because – I have my reasons," Eva growled. "I'm powerless to do anything but remind you of your place."

"I know my place. I have no illusions. And why would he want someone as broken as I am?"

"To their kind, what you've lost holds little value. Now drink your juice. I put it in the refrigerator."

"Maybe I don't want that damn tomato juice today." Rebecca wanted it badly yet hated how Eva dictated her life. "Maybe I want orange juice."

"Now, you know what the doctor said. You need the tomato juice to keep you strong." Eva stood and inspected Rebecca's face. It made Rebecca suspicious. "How are you feeling today? You didn't eat here last night. Did he take you out? What did you have?"

"Now you're concerned about my diet? Why can't you just

leave me alone?"

Rebecca turned to leave.

"He left this for you," Eva said.

Rebecca turned back to see a bright, yellow-wrapped box in Eva's bony hands. Rebecca stared at it for a moment.

"He's gone already?" Rebecca asked, feeling her heart drop into her stomach.

"He left early this morning on the redeye for London with Timothy and Roger."

"Oh," she replied. "Did he say when he'd return?"

"No." Eva's abrupt answer was like an additional knife cutting into her heart.

I didn't get to say goodbye.

"Think again if you think he'll choose you," Eva said. "He'll want a woman of status, not a clumsy housekeeper. This trinket is your only reward for your short affair. I'd never sexually contaminate myself with one of *them*. He's worse than a man-whore with all those escorts."

"Yet, you let him sample your blood the moment he arrives," Rebecca snapped. She couldn't stop it from rolling out of her. "And covet his venom like a drug addict. Get off your damn pedestal, Eva. Just because you don't partake in the Crumbs doesn't make you better than any of us. And you're like every other female here – you're in love with him and jealous of me because I was with him."

Eva stormed off. Rebecca didn't know if she walked off in embarrassment, shock or anger.

Telling that old crow off sure felt good.

Though disappointed, Rebecca opened the neatly wrapped box. She took the paper away from what it covered to find a cell phone.

***

The cell phone instructions were easy to understand, and soon, she tried out all the gadgets. She found music and the earbuds, how to surf, and soon it became her favorite toy. While at the table, in her room, bathing, or working, Rebecca found a reason or a way to use it. The phone's arrival lessened her lonely moments, and its wonderful noise-covering music drowned out Eva's constant badgering.

It opened up her world to life outside of the four walls of the manor without leaving. Now, she didn't need to experience everything firsthand. She learned of the current age, culture, technology, and world events, while the latest music intrigued her.

The phone unexpectedly rang while Rebecca listened to music. The vibration startled her, and she dropped it. Devlin's face appeared in a circle. She touched the green button on the screen.

"Hello?" she asked, her voice quivered.

"Rebecca?" Devlin's sweet voice asked. "Or, I should say, Miss Bellows?"

"Hi," she replied.

"How are you? I see you got the phone working."

"Yes, thank you," she said as her voice fluctuated excitedly. "It's incredible. I'm so sorry. I didn't think to thank you sooner."

"So, you never called anyone on it?"

"Who do I have to call?" she asked. "Everyone I once knew is dead. And everyone I know now lives in this house."

"You can call me."

"I would like to, but you're a very busy man," Rebecca said. "I don't want to be a distraction to you. You do very important work."

Devlin remained quiet, and she was compelled by the discomfort of the silence to continue. "I mean, I won't presume what happened was – more than it was. You don't owe me…."

"I know I don't," he snapped. "But we shared something special – at least to me. And I'm grateful."

"I feel that way too," she replied. "Then you should just tell me that. I like the gift, but you disappeared without a word, not even a goodbye."

"That bothered you?"

"A little," she lied because it bothered her much more. "I thought that, to you, it meant nothing. I'm just a housekeeper, and you're someone of significance. And I can accept that, but the phone confused me. Don't get me wrong, I love it. And it aggravates Madam Eva, which makes it even better."

Rebecca heard him laugh in the background.

"We don't leave the house much," she said. "And this has opened up the world in this era for me. I really do appreciate it. I'm learning so much."

"You like to learn?" he asked. "That's right, you were the one who suggested a learning budget."

"Yes," she replied. "That was me."

"When I return in a week, I'll bring you another present."

"That isn't necessary." Rebecca rolled on her bed, feeling admired. "Seeing you would be enough."

"Really?" Devlin's voice changed. "So, even if I shag you like I did before and would have to leave again...?"

Rebecca felt a thrill race up her spine and aroused in those indecent to speak of places. "Especially then."

"Good, I'll be there tomorrow."

"But you just said a week?"

"I changed my mind," Devlin replied. "I'm expected in Milan, but it can wait. I want to see you."

"I'll be here waiting," Rebecca replied, smiling from ear to ear. "I'm not going anywhere."

"I have to go. See you tomorrow," Devlin paused. "Cheers, love."

"Goodbye."

***

The following day, Rebecca dressed, completed her chores, and waited for Devlin to arrive. Every car that pulled up to the curb or the park across the street grabbed her attention. This behavior didn't escape Eva's watchful eyes.

"Do you really think he cares for you?" Eva said curtly. "Does he even know who you are, or were?"

"He does. He called me. And he said he would come."

"I have not heard of it, and if I don't hear of it, it doesn't happen."

"Maybe you're wrong this time."

"I'm never wrong." Eva marched away.

Chapter 14

Disappointment

Morning turned to evening, and Devlin still hadn't arrived. A knock at the front door and Rebecca answered it immediately. A delivery man held a box in his hand. She received it disappointedly. About the size of a medium piece of luggage. She carried it to the kitchen where Eva sat at a small desk in the corner, looking over ledger paper and scribbling with pencil, then erasing often. The paper thinned to nearly transparent and ripped with her last correction.

"Damn, now I have to start over," Eva muttered.

Eva turned when Rebecca placed the box on the table and sighed deeply. Her smug expression made Rebecca hate her for being right.

"I told you," Eva said. "I'm usually the first one to know when he's coming and going. You must have mis-understood him."

Rebecca put the box on the long oak table. Her disappointment was apparent.

"Who is the delivery for?" Eva asked.

"I don't know." Rebecca left and started for the stairs when she heard another servant's voice from the kitchen.

"Get a grip, Eva, you can be a real bitch," Gretta said.

Rebecca walked up the three flights of stairs to her little room only large enough for a tiny bed and a dresser. The wallpaper had faded, and seen better days. Rebecca spent too little time in there to notice until today. She shared the feeling of neglect that the wallpaper would if it could feel. Only a moment later, a knock at the door drew her attention. Opening it, Eva stood in the doorway holding the box, out of breath.

"Those stairs seem longer every year," Eva muttered. "It's for you."

Eva handed the box to Rebecca. Rebecca tossed it on the bed, then sat beside it, her fingers toying with a torn corner as she stared out the window. She wanted to cry, but knew better than to do that in front of Eva. She dared to hope, and now they were dashed.

"Well, aren't you going to open it?" Eva asked.

"I don't care. I wanted to see him. I don't care about his presents."

"Well, I'll open it." Eva found a pair of scissors on the dresser. She sliced the top, then along the sides carefully.

Rebecca watched the traffic moving in the street below. She heard the box open and Eva gasped. Some writing on the outside of the box caught Rebecca's glance. It read the name of a computer brand, which she recognized. It was a silver, metallic-looking rectangle immersed in foam peanuts that Eva tossed on the bed as she unearthed it. Carefully, Rebecca removed the packing.

"What do I need this for?" Rebecca asked, sitting it on her

lap. She lifted the top to open it. There, a note lay on the shallow keys.

Rebecca,

I'm sorry that I couldn't make it today, love. Urgent matters called me away. But I'll see you this weekend. Have fun with this till then.

Devlin.

"He says he will be here this weekend." She handed the note to Eva.

"I told you. He's an important man. He has so many that depend on him that he can't just fly here to see you."

"I know." Rebecca frowned. "He'll be here in only a few days."

"I wouldn't count on it," Eva replied sharply.

But when the weekend arrived, Devlin had not. Rebecca sat in the library reading when Eva found her. Eva held yet another trinket of Devlin's affection. Rebecca opened it to find a gold chain with a heart pendent. Eva handed her the envelope.

Dear sweet Rebecca,

Again, how sorry I am that I can't feel your touch or bask in the light of your countenance. But soon I'll be back. In two weeks, which would be my normal time to visit, I should be there, if not before.

Love Devlin.

Eva pulled it from the box and placed it around Rebecca's neck. Rebecca moved the curtain and took up her traffic-watching. As lovely as the gift was, she wanted to see Devlin more than anything. And this gift reminded her that she was low on his priorities. After several moments, she turned to see Eva watching her.

"You love him, don't you?" Eva asked.

"No," Rebecca snapped. "I just wanted him to keep his word this time." But she couldn't hold the lie and burst into tears. "Yes, I tried not to, and it wasn't the sex. I loved him before that."

"I'm sorry."

"Why do you even care? This only means you're right."

"I truly am sorry," she repeated with even more sincerity. "I know how a little attention from the master can make a woman crazy in love with him. But you have handled it gracefully. You're loyal without the venom and smart. Much smarter than I've been."

"So," Rebecca said, "what are smarts when you're just a housekeeper?"

"Why do you have to be just a housekeeper?"

"What else is there?" Rebecca asked.

"You know I like my shows in the evening. The television advertises these online colleges. You figured out the phone, figure out how that computer works and change your life."

"Why?"

"To be happy. You love to learn. You've practically read his entire library. But that's old knowledge, and you've thirsted for it like a dying man needs water, so educate yourself with new knowledge. This is the age for a woman to take charge of her life. Don't wait for someone to come along and hand it to you. Because it won't happen."

"You do it then," Rebecca said.

"No, I'm too old and set in my ways," Eva replied.

"But it takes money to do that. I refused my wages. I have nothing to sell or barter. Besides, I can't leave. I heard him tell you that."

Eva paused and looked around. "So, you heard all that?"

Rebecca nodded.

"Then you heard the master approved your suggestions. Whatever exceeds his limit, I'll find from the house budget."

"Why would you help me?" Rebecca asked. "You hate me."

"I don't hate you." Eva leaned against the window frame and picked at the lace curtain. "I envy you. You're not like the rest of them, the Familiars."

"What *is* a Familiar?" Rebecca asked.

"A Familiar is a servant overwhelmed by some unknown force to serve *their kind,*" Eva said. "They long to be part of *their* world and are stupidly happy to serve. But *they* don't choose Familiars to be their wives or mistresses.

"But I won't take the blame," Eva said. "You hid yourself in that kitchen, afraid to face him. That's on you. And if it's any consolation, I thought he'd be here today, too. This isn't like him. And yes, I was jealous you slept with him. I said things I shouldn't have."

"Why would you be jealous of me? I'm nobody."

"Because I was in love with him too. But he never looked at me like he does you," Eva said as a softer side appeared on her face. "Devlin was a Red Coat when we met. He didn't condone that the British set fire to Boston. He found me crying as I watched my house engulfed in flames with my husband and son trapped inside. I was only twenty years old. Devlin took pity on me. But before he rescued them, he made me choose: to die by his hand or serve him. Either way, I would be separated from my family forever. I chose the latter. He entered the burning house. The next time I saw him, he leaped from the second-story window to the ground with each one over his shoulders. I knew at that moment he wasn't a normal man. He swept me away that night, and I never saw my family again. But I knew they survived the fire and the war. I don't regret my decision. But over the years, you develop a fondness for those you serve. None of the Familiars ever did that for me, but Devlin…"

"Do you still love him?" Rebecca asked.

"Yes, when I was younger, it was a romantic type of love, but now, it's more of a motherly affection." Eva sighed. "I'd still die to keep his secrets or to make him happy. I've helped you because I know, one day, you'd make him happy."

Rebecca felt the necklace about her neck.

"Just think about what you could be," Eva said, moving toward the door. "You write, become a writer."

Surprised, Rebecca's head rose to meet the woman's eyes.

"Yes, I knew," Eva said. "There isn't much that goes on in this house that I don't know about."

"Why didn't you say something?" Rebecca asked.

"It's a hobby until you're published. Become an accountant or a lawyer. Just don't accept life on the terms it's handed you. Change and grow. Or hell, take my place for all I care. I won't live forever. And Devlin's been telling me to move into the twentieth century for ages, but I'm too old. Just consider the possibilities, the benefits you'd bring to the estate here."

"What about the master?" Rebecca asked. "I might have to leave to go to school."

"He's busy and hardly makes an appearance but once a month," Eva said. "Don't assume he'll come back for you and decide to wait. I've waited my life time and he's never looked at me like he has you. But don't waste the time; redeem it. Do something you can be proud of just in case he never shows interest again. Don't continue to be a fool as I was, waiting for something that'll never happen."

Eva closed the door behind her. Rebecca turned back to the window to watch the tiny people scurrying to their destiny, and began to dream.

Chapter 15

2016

Two years later, Rebecca poured over her lessons as the house stilled for the evening. Echoes from the kitchen signified the conclusion of dinner while the dishes clanked as they were put away. She didn't join them anymore for meals. Since the affair with the master, she became even more an outsider. She found out some time later that Devlin frequented New York, but stayed at hotels instead of the estate. And the staff blamed her for that.

Cleaning the day through, then courses by internet at night, kept her almost too busy to think of Devlin. But she did. Smelling his cologne still caught her breath, even though he had avoided the house for almost two years.

Madam Eva appeared in the doorway carrying a tray. She sat it down on the table beside Rebecca.

"Spaghetti again?" Rebecca asked. "Leftovers or new?"

"Leftovers, again," Eva said. "You can't keep sulking over the master, Becca."

"I'm not sulking. I'm busy. You don't know what it takes to have a 4.0 average."

"I'm sure I don't even know what that means." Eva paused in the doorway. "I need to tell you something."

"I have a question before you go and I forget again," Rebecca said. "While entering the data from your ledger sheets, I noticed a withdraw last month for 5 thousand dollars. Before this was only a couple of thousand per month. What is this for?"

"It's a – life insurance policy," Eva said. "For long-term care."

"How long have we been purchasing this? It might be a good time to shop better prices with this sudden rise."

"The Great Depression is when I started it. Insurance was all the rave. And I've been dealing with the same company since then. They prefer I pay in cash."

"Does Dev – the master know about this?"

"He must, he's never questioned me about it." Eva hesitated and appeared cross. "Perhaps it wasn't a good idea to make this change now. You have so much to do with school and work. I can keep doing the books."

"I'm not *that* busy," Rebecca said. She didn't look up from her typing. "I just asked a question. You don't have to get defensive." There was a long silence. "What did you want to tell me?"

"He's getting married," Eva said.

Rebecca froze, her hands hovered over the keys and every thought she had been thinking vanished.

"Are you alright?" Eva asked.

"Fine." She looked up at Eva. But instead of feeling the loss, Rebecca went numb. "He used me and now he's marrying another. You were right, as always. I started up his libido and I have lived to regret it. But I can't change it. Just shows you it wasn't love."

"It took you seventy-years to finally face him, and you act like you feel nothing? I don't know why he's doing this, but I know he loves you. When you were sick, he used to stare out the window at the park for hours so that he could be close to you to suckle when you needed him. He read to you and kept wiping your brow during the fevers. He could've assigned one of us to do it. And later, when he couldn't find you…"

"He didn't look far enough," Rebecca snipped.

"And after you returned but hid in the kitchen, he would stare out that same window for hours, then sit by the bed, like he did with you. And I could tell by the look on his face he missed you. He does love you."

"But it doesn't matter since he's marrying someone else."

Eva nodded. Rebecca noticed her face had aged years since Devlin had suckled on her.

"Are you alright?" Rebecca asked.

"Fine," Eva said. "Why do you ask?"

"No reason," Rebecca returned to the computer screen but couldn't focus. "Did he say to whom?"

"Some fashion model type," Eva said. "You know, the ones who want to stay thin and beautiful forever."

"I need to get back to work," Rebecca said but her voice

faltered.

"I'm sorry I disturbed you," Eva said, closing the door behind her.

Rebecca sat there for more moments than she thought she had. The clock struck ten when she finally woke from her daze. Tears dribbled down her cheeks, and she buried her head in her arms, weeping.

***

A year later, Rebecca sat in the same library, dressed in slacks and a business suit jacket, as her fingers floating over the keyboard, making a clacking sound. A new computer desk replaced the antique gold in-lay one that had been there for decades. She sipped on her tomato juice and balanced the accounting for the manor, when the desk phone rang.

"Good morning, Englewood Manor," Rebecca answered. "Mistress Bellows speaking."

"Ah, I need to speak to Madam Eva?" a strange voice asked. Rebecca knew the sound of a native New Yorker.

"She's ill and can't come to the phone," Rebecca informed. "I'm her assistant; how can I help you?"

"Ah, tell her the shipment is ready." There was a pause.

"Alright, anything else? Should I tell her anything else?"

"The price is five thousand and Carmichael can meet me at the last place."

"I can send Carmichael today for the pickup," Rebecca said. "Will that be sufficient?"

"I'm off at five. He knows where to meet me at six."

"We will see you…"

The phone disconnected.

***

Rebecca and Carmichael spent all day running errands for Eva. Parking at a premium, Rebecca did all the leg work. Stop after stop, Carmichael sat idling in the street as passersby stared at the 1960 Phantom Rolls. In pristine condition, it deserved the attention. The car's trunk was full of groceries, dry cleaning, liquor, and other odds and ends that kept the manor functional. At the end of the day, Rebecca reminded Carmichael of their last stop.

"I know the place," Carmichael said. "But it's a shady part of town. Promise me you'll stay in the car?"

"Alright," Rebecca replied.

"Maybe we can go for a drink later?"

"No, we need to return home. I'm feeling rather tired."

The car stopped at a light.

"This car draws too much attention." Carmichael leaned close to Rebecca, she flinched, and pulled her legs away. He reached past her into the glove compartment and withdrew a snub-nosed 38. Rebecca recognized it from the movies.

"Though I'd like very much to repeat that night," Carmichael said. "I'm not thinking about *that* just now."

"Good, don't, and stop suggesting it," Rebecca watched as he sat back behind the wheel and checked the bullets. "Has it come to this?"

Her eyes locked on his. Carmichael's handsome smile faded for a serious gaze. He snapped the cylinder back into the gun and sat it on the seat between them.

"We lead a sheltered life at the manor," Carmichael said, and the light changed. "The world is changing, but we remain the same."

The Phantom turned several corners, and they descended into more shadows each time. At every stop, a new homeless man with a spray bottle smeared a dirty rag on the windshield as Carmichael fussed or yelled at them until it became opaque with dirt. He had to engage his wipers to see. Under the bridge, Rebecca cracked the window to smell the waterfront. But fumes from the exhaust and the City Waste Authority close by made her retreat and put the vent on re-circulate.

The sky grew darker. The car stopped as its headlights fell on an old, beat-up tan Civic. From the car, a black man with white hair, looking early sixties, stepped out. Rebecca watched as Carmichael crossed in the headlights to meet the man. They exchanged words. Carmichael nodded a few times and handed the money envelope to the man in return for a white Styrofoam square box. The black man immediately jumped back into his car and sped away.

Before Carmichael could reach the car, two men stepped out of the shadows; one on Rebecca's side as another met Carmichael at the driver's door. The one man beside Rebecca attempted to open her door, but she grabbed it quick and locked it. The other held a knife on Carmichael that she could see through the window. Before the headlights, movement around them drew her attention as other vagabonds emerged.

"Give me the box," the one before Carmichael demanded. Carmichael handed it to the man who opened the lid. "What the hell is this?"

"Give him the keys to the car," the other man on Rebecca's side said.

The first thief dropped the box and held out his hand.

"They're in the ignition," Carmichael said, then took two steps back. Reaching behind him, he pulled out the gun from his pants. "Back off. Get! Before I make you into Swiss cheese."

Carmichael pointed the gun at the two men, who promptly ran off. Then he waved it at anything that moved while he picked up the package and the fallen contents. He opened the door, tossed the lid in first, and handed the rest to Rebecca. She put the lid on top, but not before she saw inside. Carmichael wasted no time driving them out from under the bridge.

"That was close," Carmichael said as the sun flickered in the windows again.

"Has that ever happened before?" Rebecca asked.

"No, they're usually too timid to approach the car. Madam has used this location several times. I guess they're becoming braver."

"Or more desperate." She pulled one of the bags from the box. Within, a red fluid moved freely. "What are these?"

"Intravenous blood bags, like hospitals use," Carmichael said. Rebecca gave him a confused look. "What! I watch a lot of medical mini-dramas."

"Why would Madam buy these for the master? He has the staff to suckle from and his special deliveries?" Then she swallowed hard as her stomach wrenched.

"Maybe it's the equivalent of a packed lunch for when he leaves?"

"We could process this ourselves. We have the mortuary table and all the supplies. We would only need to increase the number of deliveries."

"Maybe we can't. Or maybe it's more cost-effective…"

"It's not. I know what the special deliveries cost. And it's nothing close to the price of these bags."

"You know better than me. You see the books." Carmichael pointed to the box. "But I know this blood is cleaned and tested."

"There has to be another reason." Rebecca packed it away hastily.

"Madam doesn't partake at the Crumbs. Is she doing it behind everyone's back? Maybe she's so paranoid that she wants only clean blood."

"No, I can't see her doing that."

"Maybe Lord Devlin's sick and needs the processed blood."

"How long have you been doing this?" Rebecca placed the container behind the seat hoping to forget about it.

"A very long time. I didn't know what I picked up before this. I didn't pry into her business."

"I'm surprised she didn't tell me. Unless … he told her not

to." Rebecca's brow knit as she worried. *Could Devlin be dyeing?*

"It hasn't always been the same man, you know?" Carmichael stopped at a light. "Through the years, she's had to buy it from other sources. And it looks like she'll need to start looking again. He said this was the last he could get for her. He said something about not being able to fudge the books and going digital."

"That doesn't sound good."

"I asked him if he could refer anyone." Carmichael started off again when the light turned green. "He said to try outside the city."

Rebecca fell silent as she wondered and worried about Devlin.

Could this have accounted for Devlin's withdraw from the household?

Chapter 16

The Crumb's in Baggies

Rebecca knocked on Eva's bedroom door. With no answer, she knocked again. Eva beckoned for her to enter, her voice weak. Rebecca held the Styrofoam box under her arm, a box of tissues, and the master's dry cleaning in her other hand. When she opened the door, Eva propped herself up in the bed. Beside her was a nearly empty box and a pile of used tissues on the other side.

"How are you feeling?" Rebecca asked, laying the clothes over a chair.

"Better," Eva said. "But I'm just so tired."

"We picked up everything you said we needed, but it's rough out there." Rebecca held up the Styrofoam box. "We almost got mugged when we retrieved this. It goes down to the dungeon, doesn't it?"

"No, leave it with me," Eva snapped.

"But it needs to be refrigerated."

"Then here." Eva pulled a chain from around her neck and handed it to Rebecca. "Make yourself useful."

Rebecca took it as Eva pointed to a small red refrigerator

beneath her desk. She unlocked the small refrigerator, revealing several of the same kind of blood bags within. Placing them in the tray, she moved the oldest to the front.

"Are you expecting the master soon?" Rebecca asked.

"No."

"But this supply of blood will expire soon, probably before he comes."

"He's not the one I buy them for," Eva muttered.

"What?" Rebecca said, noticing the can of tomato juice before she closed the door. "Then who...?"

Since Eva's been sick, I've not been served tomato juice with my breakfast. Strange that there is no tomato juice in the house except here. Very strange.

"I thought you didn't like tomato juice?" Rebecca asked, relocking the refrigerator door.

"I hate it," Eva muttered again.

"Then why do you have it in this refrigerator if ...?" Rebecca realized something dreadful. She felt acid from her stomach back up into her mouth, and she clamped her hand over her lips. "This blood is for me? You've been spiking my juice with—how could you?"

"You don't understand," Eva said hastily, trying to sit up. The act of exertion caused her to cough harder. Blood spotted the tissue she held to her lips.

"You couldn't stand that I didn't partake with the others in the Crumbs, so you were mixing blood into my food?"

"No, that is not why," Eva returned to the pillow. "Let me

explain."

"I can't believe you'd do such a thing." Rebecca held her stomach as it churned, and she sank to the floor while her mind emptied of all other thoughts.

"Doctor Wells needed time to work on you," Eva began. "The venom slowed your heart rate and thereby slowed your bleeding. Devlin suckled on you to keep you unconscious, calm, and alive. He saved your life with his venom, but at a cost. I didn't know that he was in love with you at the time, but he worked to keep you alive all those weeks, then it turned to months with the high fevers. Doctor Wells thought you were hemorrhaging because the fevers were so high. And Devlin continued to suckle. Then you went missing, and Devlin searched for you. That's when I realized he loved you.

"When you returned from the hospital, you didn't gain weight. You were always weak, cold, and frail. Your skin hung on you like mine does now. You looked like you were starving, yet you ate the same food as we did, even larger portions, but nothing helped. But I had a feeling.

"Through a phone call to St. Petersburg, I found out it takes up to four months of suckling for a woman to be turned into one of *them*, according to the servants. But someone isn't considered a vampire until they've fed for the first time. It's the process they do when a wife is chosen. They said many of the women died of high fevers, which you had." Eva breathed heavily. "I wondered when you'd find out. I knew I couldn't keep the secret forever. I wanted to tell you, but I feared what you'd do if you knew."

Rebecca's horror increased as she remembered while shock kept her glued to the floor. She couldn't fathom her own despair. "You're lying to me. I'm perfectly fine. I don't need that."

"You know you do. Tell me, have you been more tired lately. And food without the blood isn't satisfying you, is it?" Eva took a deep breath. "At least now I don't have to lie anymore."

"This was your insurance policy, wasn't it? Long-term care I think you called it."

"I didn't do it just for you." Eva stared at the ceiling. "I feared what you would do to the others if you starved. So, I took it upon myself to slip blood into everything that had a tomato base. And look at you. Your beauty was restored, as was your stamina. He turned you into one of them by accident." Eva looked even more pale and tired.

"That's impossible." Rebecca shook her head. "I don't have fangs, I'm not strong or fast, and I don't crave blood; in fact, it makes me sick to my stomach; I'm nothing like *them*. You have to be mistaken."

But I've been feeling weaker lately. No wonder everything tastes odd; she's not spiking my food. I crave the damn tomato juice even though I hate it. Can it be true?

Rebecca began to cry as she couldn't deny her new reality. "You know how I felt about this, why didn't you just let me die?"

"Because he loved you," Eva said. "And you loved him, or you wouldn't have returned to us. I wanted to tell him you lived when you came back, but you were so sickly. I saw how losing you the first time almost destroyed him. If you died again, I worried for his sanity, so I waited to see if you'd recover. When you did, you were so broken and in despair. I wanted to tell him, but you asked me not to. I thought if I gave you a little more time, you'd come around. But you didn't. He moved on and you seemed content, so I left the whole damn thing alone. And don't blame me. You've lived under his roof and could have reentered his life at any time. When you both rediscovered each other, I thought he'd take you for a wife then."

"He led me on for almost a year, but I can't stay angry with you. Had it not been for you, I would've wallowed in self-pity. You risked being discovered... for me? But now he's engaged to be married. He doesn't love me and all this has been a waste."

"You don't know him like I do. For the first two years, he asked about you every time he called. When he came here and stayed in hotels, I'd go out to meet him. Carmichael was told not to tell you as well. I hid your sorrow from him, as I hid his from you. I didn't think it would help you move on. But I've seen this before; their kind aren't the most intuitive where love is concerned. I thought he'd return for you, but when he announced his engagement, I told him he made a mistake. I told him of your sorrow and how you turned bitter."

"You told him that?" Rebecca shook her head. "If he still loves me, why has he withdrawn from me?"

"He never told me why when I asked," Eva said. "But there is more I need to tell you. The servants in the other households called your condition "unsettled". You're not one of us anymore, but you're not quite one of them either. You can't feed on a human, or you'll turn the rest of the way. Those bags are for you, use them wisely. But beware, too much could push you over the edge. Too little may create a hunger you can't control."

"This situation might not last much longer." Rebecca placed the key around her neck and rose. "This is the last shipment from this supplier. They're converting to a computerized system, and he can't be creative with the accounting anymore."

"Oh, no. What will we do?"

"This isn't your problem anymore." Rebecca picked up the dry cleaning and sat the box of tissues on the bed. "I also understand why you did it, but you should have told me sooner. I can't imagine harming anyone here and I don't know if I can kill someone."

"If you get hungry enough, I'm sure that won't be an issue. What are you going to do? You can't leave."

"Find another supplier, if I can," Rebecca said. "But that's a band-aid solution. And what if Devlin finds out? I remember him saying once that his family has to come into agreement before a woman is changed. There'll be consequences for this."

"Then I suggest you keep this a secret—from everyone."

Chapter 17

Unsettling Change

Two months later, on the next grocery run, Carmichael held the door open to the Rolls while Rebecca placed the last of the paper bags in the back seat. Just before she stooped to enter, Carmichael let go of the door and pressed his body against hers, his hands on either side to keep her from moving. She leaned back against the car to maintain the distance between their upper bodies until she couldn't.

"Let go," Rebecca said. She pushed him as he leaned in for a kiss. She turned her face away. "Don't make me hurt you."

"Becca, it's been almost a year since our affair," Carmichael said as he eased back but didn't relinquish her freedom. "And you just dodge the subject or avoid me. You never gave me a reason we broke up."

"An affair? Is that what you've been telling everyone?" Rebecca let out a discouraging chuckle. "It was a tryst, a moment of passion in the back of the car. Not even enough to call it a one-night stand. Nothing happened."

"It's because I couldn't make you – you know," Carmichael stuttered. "And you won't give me another chance to make love to you."

"I was half lit and so were you." She shook her head. "This has nothing to do with sexual satisfaction."

"Then tell me why?"

"I was too busy with school before," she lied.

"And now?"

"And now I'm moving up in the house." She looked at his chest to avoid his eyes. "And you're still the chauffeur. The others would think I have favoritism for you."

"That's bullshit," Carmichael said.

Rebecca thought for a moment and realized she lied to save his feelings from being hurt. But he hurt with her excuses, too. Her reasons made her feel superior. The manor's strong class structure made for a good scapegoat. For Rebecca, the truth was harder to admit. She still loved Devlin.

"You're right," Rebecca said. "The truth is, on the first day I arrived here, you practically drooled over me while I lay bleeding. And that look has not left you when you look at me now. I tried to ignore it because we grew up in the same time, held the same values, liked some of the same things, and I thought we were friends. But you still look at me as if you want to eat me."

"I do." Carmichael smiled with a hungry look in his eyes as they traveled south to her V-neck sweater where her cleavage began. "But it's not your blood now I want."

"That's not love but lust."

"No, I have feelings for you. And I can *do* better. I can *be* better."

"But I don't have feelings for you," Rebecca replied sympathetic and in a quiet tone. "You'll always be my friend, but nothing more."

"You still love him, don't you?"

"That's none of your business," she snipped.

Carmichael leaned in and slammed his fist against the top of the Rolls. She flinched at his anger. "Damn it, Rebecca. He's marrying another. What was I, your rebound?"

"No," she replied. "I wanted to move on, but I can't. I didn't mean to lead you on. I'm sorry."

Nearly a year had passed since she found out, and she delt with it internally. Only Eva knew her real struggles. From the staff she distanced herself with her new authority and, like Eva, became stoic in her emotions. The tryst with Carmichael had been her only attempt to move on. And when it failed, she resigned herself to being alone.

Then he softened. "I think often if you and I – would have been together before him, things would now be different."

"You never noticed me before Devlin," she replied.

"Why can't I love you?" Carmichael asked. "Why won't you let me?"

"Because I can't love you in return," she said. "And it would be cruel of me to let you. Resign yourself to the fact that we aren't going to be together, and I won't let *that* happen again."

With downcast eyes, Carmichael grabbed the door frame,

took a step back, and nodded. The truth had been long overdue, but she hated to hurt him. She only hoped the truth would free him to find another.

Carmichael climbed in the front as Rebecca slipped into the back of the car and took her seat on the bench below the dividing window. An awkward silence presided between them for some time.

The rest of the car was stacked with boxes of booze, bags of groceries, large blocks of paper goods, dry cleaning, and other supplies that filled the back seat and trunk. Carmichael departed for home after their long day of shopping. He knew the streets of New York City better than any digital mapping system. Rebecca studied her to do list until the car had been stopped for a while.

"What's wrong?" she asked, breaking the silence.

"Looks like an accident." Carmichael inched forward and blared the horn, then nudged into the intersection. "I'll head down 91st Avenue and try to maneuver around it."

"Good, I want to return with Madam Eva's new medication as quickly as possible."

"I'm going to miss New York City." He turned right at the next street and the traffic flowed better. "Nothing like walking down the street for a beer, a taco, and a slice of pizza, all on the same block."

"I know. I've never lived outside the city before. This has always been my home. But times are changing. The neighborhood doesn't feel safe after the shooting across the street in the park. Frieda still won't take the garbage to the dumpster since that homeless man scaled the fence and tried to take advantage of her."

"This car doesn't help matters," Carmichael replied. "I remember when I could leave the windows down and talk to anyone without fear. Now, I feel like a target. And the old neighborhoods aren't like when we were young."

"New York has always had its share of violence."

"Would you tell the Madam that it's difficult to find replacement parts for this car? This thing's a museum piece. We need something more modern."

"The sooner we arrive home, the sooner we can put the car away. This car won't seem so out of place in the country where the new house is. But you're right, we should purchase something smaller and more fuel efficient for our shopping days. Then, you'll only have to drive this relic to pick up the master."

"Any word on his return?"

"No, madam Eva has not heard anything from him in over a month."

"I like shopping with you better than Eva." Carmichael lowered his voice. "She's not doing well, is she?"

"No, she's not," Rebecca said. "All her responsibilities fall on me now. I think everyone knows Eva's not going to get better no matter how she puts on a good show."

"We all have to go sometime," Carmichael said. But Rebecca could hear the hesitance in his voice. "Suckling won't keep us from the Grim Reaper forever."

On the eve of the transition to the new manor, Eva's illness

157

adversely affected the household. Moving would only solve some of their problems, but not Eva's. The thoughts of Eva's longevity, suckling, and her own condition, weighed heavily on her among all the other changes the household faced.

How much time do I have since I'm not really human now? One day, they'll know. Carmichael won't care. Or he'll be envious. He'd jump at the chance to become one of them.

Carmichael turned the car to the right, where a sign read: "Detour". A few blocks more, and Rebecca noticed the dismal state of the neighborhood. They passed mattresses left at the street curb, cars on cement blocks, and graffiti-covered buildings. Men sat on the front stoops of apartment buildings whose windows had bars. She could smell ganja.

"I think we took a wrong turn," Rebecca said.

Carmichael pointed to tagging on the cars and houses. "This is gang territory."

"Like the gangsters, the mob?" Rebecca asked.

"Yeah, kind of, they call it turf wars. I saw movies about it. But not like the organized crime we saw in our day. The ones with red neckerchiefs fight those who wear blue, and they call themselves Bloods or Crips."

"Like Romeo and Juliet or West Side Story?"

"Yeah, only with semi-automatics."

They stopped at a T-intersection. Looking right, then left, neither way looked promising to Rebecca. She saw two men approaching Carmichael's side of the car out of the corner of her eye.

Carmichael waited for the traffic to clear, leaning hard on the stirring wheel to see, when the two figures closed in on his side. Within feet of the car door, she caught sight of a metal rod.

"Watch out," Rebecca yelled as a tire iron hit the driver-side window.

Carmichael leaned away as the glass showered him, and the bar nearly struck his face. One of the men, dressed in a long black raincoat, leaned through the window and grabbed the door handle. He yanked the door hard, and it flew open. The other man brandished a switchblade, cut Carmichael seatbelt, grabbed his jacket and pulled him from the driver's seat. The two men dragged Carmichael only a few feet away, tossed him to the street and kicked him a few times.

"Carmichael!" But Rebecca knew he couldn't hear her outside the car. She tried to get out but both side doors were locked. And she didn't have time to crawl to the front before the men returned.

The two dark-dressed men quickly moved back to the Phantom Rolls and climbed in the front. The first put the car in gear and turned left while the other emptied the glove box. Rebecca shrank among the bags and watched as Carmichael limped after the car. He shrank in size as they turned the corner. Alone with the carjackers, Rebecca realized the danger.

"We'll get this heap to the chop shop," said the driver. "And get paid a pretty penny for it."

"Andy's wanted this car for a while," said the one in the passenger side. "Hey, nice piece."

Rebecca knew he found Carmichael's gun with the sound of the barrel spin. The car made several turns. If they made it to the chop shop, her chances of negotiating her freedom would be reduced considerably.

A hard turn and Rebecca slid out of the seat. She smashed some of the paper bags, which made a horridly loud noise. Both men looked back. The passenger-side carjacker turned while the driver looked up into the rearview mirror.

"Look what we have here," the second man said.

Rebecca froze when their eyes locked, and she feared what the man might have thought.

"If you stop, I'll let you take the car with no hassles," she whispered. "I don't want trouble."

"Now why would we want to do that?" The driver looked in the mirror with a toothless grin.

The other man eyed her and produced a muffled whistle. "It's our lucky day."

"Go for it, Dan," the driver snickered.

The man in the passenger seat, Dan, crawled through the window between the car's compartments before Rebecca could raise the divider. When he reached her, he grabbed her wrist from the controls and pulled her toward him on the other seat. She landed in the corner right behind the driver. The dirty-clothed, greasy-haired man smiled lustfully. His eyes cascaded down her body as she felt he undressed her with them.

"You're a real babe," Dan said. He touched her arm, then

reached for her face. His other handheld the revolver on her.

Rebecca slapped his hand away. "Leave me alone."

"Such a fancy lady," Dan said as he continued. His hand landed on her knee at the hem of her skirt and slipped beneath it. The gun rested next to her cheek, and she tolerated his hand as it slid up under her skirt. When he reached the clamp on her garter belt, she couldn't take it any longer. Self-preservation erupted and she pushed him away. He slipped off the seat but held the gun on her still.

Rebecca smoothed her skirt down. "Don't touch me," she squeaked. Her fear paralyzed her vocal cords.

"Hey," the driver said. "Save some for me. I'll find a nice dark bridge and we'll have some fun."

Dan shoved the gun in the front of his pants then stood over her as the car weaved around traffic. He had a hard time keeping his balance while straddling her legs and attempting to pin her arms against the seat back. With a quick swipe across the face, Rebecca drove her well-painted crimson nails into the greasy pockmarked skin. The man reared back and fell among the paper bags on the back seat. Three long, bloody claw marks appeared across his cheek.

"You bitch," Dan yelled as he wiped his face with the back of his hand, painted red with his blood.

Rebecca's fingernails were covered in the red fluid. The smell of it aroused her senses like freshly cut flowers did back in the day. And the same feeling dropped to the pit of her stomach, a ravenous, churning sensation that half caused her to want to throw up. But this time, it was different. Her heart raced, mouth salivated, and her gums tingled. Her fingertips ached, but she didn't investigate as to why. She lost her inhibitions with her fixation on the man.

"What's wrong?" the driver asked.

"She scratched me," Dan said, then glared at Rebecca. "No more Mr. Nice Guy."

"Who said you were nice in any sense of the term before?" Rebecca asked.

Rebecca sat up and leaned in Dan's direction. Placing her hands on his knees, she glared at him as her lips parted, and white fangs took the place of her normal canines.

"You're the mossst grotesssque, disgusssting figure of a man," she said with a slur.

Something inside her snapped. She leapt on top of the man, whaled on him with her arms, then clawed his body like a wild beast. Dan screamed as razor-like gashes seeping blood appeared on his face, arms and neck. He attempted to block her as his anger changed to fear. He pushed her away, and she paused, inhaling deeply.

"Your fear isss a delightfully aromatic," she said as she maneuvered, countering his every move, like a mountain lion stalking a gazelle.

"Who are you?" Dan yelled. "Craig, help me. I think she's a…"

"Hey, stop that," Craig, the driver, yelled from the front seat yet continued to drive.

Rebecca grabbed the forearm that shielded Dan's face and pressed it to the back of the seat. Then, her mouth made straight for his neck, and she plunged her newly elongated fangs into his soft flesh. With one long suck, she felt the crimson flood fill her mouth. Nothing else tasted as sweet or fulfilled her being like it before. Like something lost that had been found, and she felt whole.

As she sat back, blood pulsed out all over the paper bags, down the front of the man's clothes, and squirted in her face. She rubbed her cheek and inserted her fingers into her mouth.

"Sweet, mother of god …" Rebecca snarled as the taste invigorated her appetite for more. She licked her lips and felt the points of her fangs. "I taste the essence of motor oil, but it's a hell of a lot better than tomato juice."

Dan's arms flailed as he screamed and kicked. Rebecca went back in for more, and Dan slowly ended his struggle as she sucked his life's precious blood. She felt the energy surge through her limbs and torso like lightning. In an instant, the brain fog she battled with for eighty years vanished. Nothing ever had felt like it.

"Dan, Dan," Craig, the driver called, then half turned in his seat. "What did you do to him?"

"I drank him," she said. "And you're next."

Rebecca reached for the driver, whose right arm swung aimlessly through the window divider to keep her away. She struggled with the man whose attention moved to her as she bit his arm through the window. Losing control of the car, it accelerated rapidly. Rebecca flew back against the back seat as the car turned, then straightened. It ran a red light, jumped a curb, and headed for a cement pillar under one of the bridges.

"Look out," she yelled as she drove her new claws into the seat to hold onto the metal frame.

Rebecca cringed as the car sped out of control toward the bridge support. She felt the car's back end leave the ground as the front contacted the cement buttress, then a sudden stop. Everything in the rear of the car, including Dan, flew past her into the front. Dan's body became a projectile through the windshield as it hugged him like Suran wrap. His body sprawled over the crumpled hood. The front seat wedged Craig against the steering wheel.

The back end of the vehicle dropped, and everything landed around her. Rebecca felt battered, but no broken bones. She knelt, looking through the glass divide now bent to hell. The steering wheel had impaled the driver's chest. He made gurgling noises and exhaled but never inhaled again. Dan didn't move either as Rebecca kicked open the rear door. She stumbled to stand for a moment as her disorientation cleared.

As the reality set in, she realized she couldn't remain by the car. Those in the stores on the block close by would begin to emerge with the sound of the accident. The police would question her about how her clothes became bloody, how the driver lost control, and her DNA would be in the wounds they sustained. All questions she couldn't face at that moment.

Rebecca grabbed her purse, the gun she spotted on the floor, and Eva's medicine from the back of the wreck. As in her day, a man carried a handkerchief for a woman, she had made it a practice to carry a lighter for a man. Grabbing a paper towel roll, Rebecca shoved it behind the front wheel and lit it with her lighter. The flames caught the paper then the leaking fuel.

As the flames enveloped the car, Rebecca headed for an alley and ran, sensing newfound strength and speed like never before. The century-long confusion vanished. She felt settled, confident, and powerful. And in that moment, she realized what she had become.

Chapter 18

New Digs

A month after the carjacking, the upgrades to the new property were complete. The Manhattan Manor's staff furiously packed. Just outside of a week, they took up residence in Upper New York City, an hour outside the Lincoln tunnels.

Sunset at the new manor were vastly different from Manhattan. Brilliant orange clouds illuminated the skies behind the property that butted up to the forest. Acres of fields and trees surrounded the strange 70s-style structure. The long-slanted roof and large, thick windows on every floor exposed the inside to light all day. Those windows overlooked a small wooden pier that jutted toward the center of the lake.

Between the lake and the house was an in-ground, heated pool. The house came with a two-bay garage which Rebecca enlarged to three due to the new dungeon she buried behind it. After the destruction of the Phantom Rolls Royce, Rebecca purchased something stylish, yet practical while anticipating inclement weather. Two for the price of one, she purchased a Range Rover/limo and a go-to-town SUV. The Range Rover would be Devlin's main ride because it had been modified, slightly stretched with tinted windows, shiny black exterior, and heated seats. It sat handsomely in the new garage. Not only did Carmichael get the toy he wanted, now he had a workbench and a place to call his own. A small room off to the side, meant for a storage cabinet, became his bedroom.

Dug into the back hill, the new dungeon housed matching sarcophaguses. Rebecca had ordered a new one to be carved out of the stone from a nearby quarry. Knowing how much Devlin liked the Manhattan manor, she fashioned the new dungeon in like manner. Servant quarters had been a glorified chicken coop and barn. Renovated, the staff had their own building with a connecting subterranean tunnel that led to the main house in case of deep snow or torrential rain.

Several changes occurred with the purchase of the new estate and its renovations. The staff became insecure, which Rebecca attributed to change. The world changed around the staff, but few embraced it. Routine gave them purpose and stability. Change created chaos. But Rebecca managed them well and the new manor gave them the safety the city couldn't.

For some unknown reason, not just some, but all of the servants competed for her attention and favor. They would nag her with offers to serve her until she would grow cross with them, and fall all over themselves to follow her commands. Their strange behavior, though sweet, felt more isolating than their outright blaming her for Devlin's absence.

With her unsettling change into a vampire, Rebecca stayed in the main house, avoiding the staff. Down the hall from the master suite, she took up residence in a small child's bedroom. The staff needed her close, but their strange behavior annoyed her. Even more, she became the recluse.

Rebecca eagerly desired to experience the winters, with the rolling hills and lakes. Though she would miss the city, the countryside provided a well invited change. At times, it felt like she had forgotten something in the old manor, and it grew a little stronger each day. But the staff reassured her that they had packed everything but the kitchen sink.

Rebecca also noticed her pale complexion glistened with a youthful glow. Her hands were not as skeleton-like, yet they were colder. She went almost without sleep, even though she felt stronger and healthier. She hid her new abilities from the staff, worried they wouldn't take the change well.

But her newfound food source brought complications and guilt. She feared her appetite would exceed the blood bags. Meanwhile, the carjacking haunted her idle thoughts. And with the source of her supplies gone, she had to find a new avenue to purchase what she needed. It weighed on her mind night and day, but she told no one.

***

Rebecca entered the servant's quarters and ascended the stairs to Eva's room. Eva had grown weaker, restricted to a large bed with the covers up to her chin. She complained of being cold, though the thermostat read eighty-nine degrees.

"Mistress Rebecca," Eva muttered weakly, struggling to breathe. "You're finally back."

Rebecca turned, smiled, and sat beside her on her bed. "Are you hungry or thirsty? I can ring for Gretta to make you something."

"No, I'm not hungry," Eva snapped.

"You haven't eaten in days." Rebecca worried. "This isn't like you. How can you heal if you don't eat?"

"I'm dying, child." Eva pointed to the phone on the nightstand. "I need to call Lord Devlin."

"You can barely hold the receiver let alone dial it." Rebecca grimaced at the thought of Eva's fate. "What was the doctors last prognosis? Have you been lying to us?"

"When I was hospitalized last week from the fall, they took an MRI and I'm riddled with cancer."

That's what I smell; this must be what death smells like. Or maybe it's the cancer. Either way, she won't be with us for much longer. Wonder if I could suckle her? But could I stop?

"Are you in pain?"

"At times," Eva said. "But the doctor gives me this patch to help with the nausea and pain. I just wish the master were here. Now, before I get too tired…"

I need to tell her. I need to know what I should do. Rebecca hesitated and wrung her hands together.

"I'll dial the number," Rebecca said. "But first, I need to tell you something."

"I'm dying," Eva said, sarcastically. "What could be so

important?"

"It's about what happened with the Rolls. I have to tell someone. But you have to promise to take it to your grave."

"That won't be long. You're agitated. What's bothering you? This isn't like you."

"I didn't tell Carmichael or the police the truth about the carjacking. The men didn't stop the car and toss me out."

"They raped you?" Eva's voice filled with concern. "Oh, my dear…"

"No, I didn't give him the chance, though one tried. I—fed— for the first time."

Eva laughed which turned to coughing, and nodded, as if the news didn't shock her.

"They deserved as much," she growled. "That car was a classic. Well, you're no longer unsettled, and there is no going back. I should have known. Everything about your appearance enhanced. But you have a hungry look in your eyes; go and satisfy yourself. Devlin can wait a bit longer."

Rebecca removed one of the blood bags from the small red refrigerator. Taking it to the adjacent bathroom, she punctured it with scissors. The moment she smelled the blood, she felt her mouth water, her body tense, her canines lengthen. Her desire overwhelmed her self-control. Looking in the mirror, her dark blue eyes turned black for only a moment.

She sucked the bag straight down. Resting momentarily at the sink, she felt despair and self-loathing. When consumed, her strength renewed, her mind cleared, and the emptiness in her stomach satisfied.

What have I become? The very thing I couldn't stomach. It's wrong, but I feel so good for the first time in decades. I'm not human now, I'm one of them. Do they all feel like this? Does Devlin?

Rebecca returned to Eva's bedside. The sick woman had dozed off, but only for a few moments. Eva had aged as if overnight. Her skin sagged like the bones beneath had shrunk and her skin turned ashen color.

"You're back," Eva said. "That didn't take long."

"What if I can't control this?" Rebecca asked. "I can't stay here. I can't risk hurting anyone."

"But you can't leave now." Eva coughed when she spoke. "I need you. Lord Devlin will need you. Who will care for the staff and Lord Devlin when I'm gone?"

"Lord Devlin is getting married. Do you think I want to be around for that?"

"You can't move past it, can you? You're still in love with him?"

"Yes. I've tried to move on, but it didn't change anything. Now I'm just angry and bitter."

"I know your pain, 243 years. But you, you were special to him. He wouldn't let you die. I was jealous when you slept with him. And I really thought he'd come back for you. But when he didn't, I saw the same look in your eyes as in my own. That's why I pushed you to go to school. I don't know why he didn't choose you for a wife. But I guess it's too late to speculate now. Just promise me you'll help him with the transfer to another head housekeeper before you leave."

"I promise you that." Rebecca hesitated. "But you told me not to let anyone know. I can't hide that I want to feed anymore. He's bound to find out. How can I remain here?"

"I'll see if I can persuade him to let you go or find a position in one of his companies," Eva said. "He may understand your awkward situation with his future wife and make an exception for you. Maybe a position in one of the other family's properties. But you must not tell him that you turned. The other servants were adamant that the uncles would never allow an unsanctioned vampire to exist. You feed too carelessly, and they'll find you. It won't be any easier there as it is here."

"I know."

Eva attempted to pull herself up on the pillows, then fell back as if it took all her strength. Rebecca slid her hands into Eva's armpits and lifted her effortlessly higher up in the bed. Her strength would at least be practical in Eva's condition.

"I want to thank you, Eva," Rebecca began. "If it hadn't been for you, I wouldn't have lived or gotten my education."

"Pish-posh," Eva muttered. "It was all your doing that has made a future for yourself."

"But I appreciate your support and I'm grateful. I wanted you to know that in case you pass in your sleep." Rebecca hesitated.

"The truth is, I saw a desire in you to better yourself.

Suggesting schooling, I wanted to prepare you to be a better match than some of the other wives. Devlin deserves a woman who would be his equal."

"Does he even know about my degree?"

"No," she said. "I never told him. Like the house, I wanted it to be a surprise. He likes surprises. At least, he used to."

"Devlin will come when he finds out your dyeing, won't he?"

"Yes," Eva paused. "He usually comes."

"If you are in pain, before he arrives, please let me know." Rebecca smiled down at her. "I have venom of my own now."

"Yes, yes," Eva waved her away, then pointed again to the rotary phone beside her bed. "Now, help me."

Rebecca handed her the receiver. But Eva had a hard time handling its weight. "Now dial his number. I know you know it."

Rebecca nodded and stroked the dial for each number with her long, red nails.

"Now leave," Eva barked. "I can't explain everything to him with you crying in the background."

Rebecca hadn't realized the tears that fell down her cheeks. She brushed them away and walked to the door, closing it softly behind her. Her tears were not for Eva alone. The thought of leaving these people and not serving Devlin seemed almost heartbreaking. This had been her only link to him, even if all it produced was painful memories.

Chapter 19

Call to Devlin

Eva didn't last the week. The soberness of the room ate at Rebecca. She sipped her coffee tinted red with blood and vowed to never allow another drop of tomato juice to cross her lips again. She stood inside the door to the kitchen having announced Eva's passing. Some of the staff sat while other stood with downcast faces. Carmichael tried to conceal it, but the tears leaked down his chiseled jaws. Some of the women couldn't hold back and wept openly.

"Why didn't the master come?" asked one of the men. "He's always come before."

"I don't know," Rebecca replied. "She called him last week to let him know and I assumed he'd come. But obviously he's busy or maybe she asked him not to."

"Why would she do that?" Elizabeth asked.

She shrugged. "Maybe she wanted to die."

Rebecca figured by the look on their faces that they still blamed her for Devlin's absence from the New York estate. Eva wanted the new residence to be a surprise, but would have had to tell Devlin. Any joy the new house provided seemed overshadowed by her death.

"She will be missed," Rebecca said.

"May she rest in peace," the staff said in unison.

"Did she say how she wanted—buried?" Gretta asked.

"Yes, she didn't want cremation. She had a fear of fire back from before she arrived here."

"When will it be?" Another asked.

"Once I know if or when the Master will arrive, we'll have the viewing and funeral. Gretta, can you get her 'Crumbs' dress drycleaned in the meantime. She specified she wanted to be buried in it."

"Yes, mum," Gretta replied.

"She left a Will to disperse her few belongings; we'll go over it once I know when the funeral will take place." Rebecca turned to go.

"Madam Eva and I had a thing, back in the day," Old Pete said with a generous smile. "She was a real bobcat back then. Is that what they call that now?"

Rebecca snickered at the thought.

"Cougar?" Carmichael asked. "Do you mean she was older than you and she seduced a younger man?"

"Yeah, I had just come to the manor after the end of the Civil War, I was 26 and she was, well, over a hundred. Sex was— incredible. But it fizzled out after a few years."

"Oooohhh," Elizabeth shivered. "TMI. There's an image I won't be able to shake for a while."

175

"When did Eva stop partaking in the Crumbs?" Rebecca asked.

"She never participated," Gretta replied. "Not that I ever remembered."

Rebecca left them in the kitchen and made her way to Eva's room. She felt the tangible grief; as if a heaviness in the air made even the most mundane tasks strenuous. She knew it would last for a few weeks as it did with other beloved servants who passed. But they were all beloved; when a group spent dozens of decades together, strong bonds formed.

She opened the door and stared out the window. Behind her lay a still body in the bed, with several quarter sized spots of blood on the pillow beside Eva's smiling face. In the end, Eva needed her venom and she felt honored to help her friend.

The sun rose over the horizon on the lake side as Rebecca watched. She paced, holding the cell phone. With all the events of the last few months like the carjacking, vagrants trespassing on the property, the move to the new estate, Eva's illness and now death, she didn't anticipate this call.

I can do this. He's getting married. He's moved on, and our past didn't mean the same to him as it did to me. Damn it, why can't I leave this behind me; this schoolgirl infatuation with a man who doesn't care. Just make the call and be done with it. But it won't be over soon. There is still the funeral and all the business with the new house. At least his fiancé will be here to distract him, and I'll be just as busy finding a replacement for the Madam. Now, make the call.

Rebecca pressed the button on her cell that brought up Devlin's smiling face. The dial tone clicked, and she could hear rustling in the background.

"Hello," Devlin said in that sweet, velvety voice. He dropped the phone and his voice became distant for a moment. "Bloody hell, hold on." There was fumbling in the background. "Hello," Devlin said, louder and clear again.

Rebecca's mouth dried, her heart ached, her throat clenched, and butterflies launched in her stomach all at once. She faltered, croaking out some unintelligent word that should have been a greeting.

"Who is this?" Devlin growled. "How did you acquire this private number? Is this a friend of Felecia? Stop leaving threatening messages on my phone. Wait, no, this number is from the States."

Rebecca cleared her throat. "Good morning, Lord Englewood. This is Mistress Bellows."

I wonder if he remembers...

"Who?" he asked. "Bellows?"

No, he doesn't.

She felt both disappointed and yet relieved. *It might be easier if he doesn't. Maybe I can be very professional and distance my feelings until this is all over.*

"I'm Madam Eva's assistant," she said.

"Rebecca—forgive me; I didn't recognize your voice. It's good to hear from you. I don't recall seeing you the last time I was in residence."

"It's been years," she replied. "Thanks to you and the Madam, I've been attending college."

"College?" Devlin asked, surprised. "Oh, that's why she chose you as her assistant."

"Were you sleeping?"

Why did I ask that? I know he wasn't. He doesn't sleep, just like I don't now.

"No, just lost in thought, distracted. I take it the Madam is still feeling poorly if she is having you ring me. Is this about my impending travel to the States?"

"Yes and no," Rebecca hesitated. "I regret to inform you that Madam Eva passed away this morning. Ahh, were you planning on returning soon?"

There was a momentary silence.

"What?" Devlin gasped. "What happened? She only called me less than a week—and, she said she would be fine. I don't understand."

"Her suffering is over, so yes, she *is* fine, *now.* She's dead."

"What did she die of?"

"Cancer," Rebecca replied. "The doctor said she had it for years. It had somehow encapsulated itself in her body. But, without the suckling, it progressed. But she didn't even tell me until she became bedridden. I'm surprised you didn't know. But you're busy with your business, and now the wedding."

"Yes, I've been busy." Devlin paused. "When is the funeral?"

"I'll find out today," she replied. "But all the arrangements have been made. The Madam arranged most of it while she could direct me as to her wishes. Will you be attending?"

"Of course," Devlin said with a ring of hostility. "I always attend funerals. Why didn't you call and tell me what was happening to her."

"She said she was going to tell you a week ago. I assumed she did. Obviously, she didn't."

"No, our last conversation was mostly about my fiancée," Devlin said. "Did she mention my plans?"

"No, sir, she didn't," Rebecca said. "I've arranged for you and your bride-to-be to board a private jet. Under the circumstances, I felt you both needed as much privacy as possible."

For the bloodthirsty bitch.

"Yes, that is very thoughtful, thank you."

"Sir, may I wish you and your fiancée the very best for the future."

There, I said it.

"Thank you, but…"

"All will be arranged for your arrival," she said, cutting him off. "You only need to text me your time of departure. Shall I prepare for two to be dining on your special diet?"

"No, just for one," Devlin hesitated. "Will you meet me at the airport? I would very much like to talk to you—privately."

"No, I don't travel in the city after dark because of the incident with the Rolls Royce."

"Oh, I'm sorry. I didn't know you were involved. Were you

hurt?"

"Please, I don't want to talk about it right now. I'll be waiting at the house for your arrival. I assume it will be on the red-eye?"

"Yes," Devlin paused. "It will take me just a bit longer to detangle myself here."

"Take your time, I'm sure the funeral home does not have a same-day service."

"That's cute. You always were witty."

Of all the things to remember; my lame sense of humor.

"Did the Madam die alone?" Devlin asked. Rebecca could hear the grief mounting in his voice. "I'm usually there to assist in a passing. I don't know why she didn't tell me. I would have flown home immediately."

"I wondered that myself, sir," she said with an accusing tone. "I thought it unusually callus of you. But she was never alone and died peacefully in her sleep."

Peacefully with my assistance.

Rebecca fought the tears.

"You've been up all night?" Devlin asked. "You must be exhausted."

"I'm fine, sir," she said, but couldn't hinder her voice from revealing her sorrow.

"Thank you for calling me."

"Goodbye, sir." Rebecca waited. There was a moment before Devlin responded.

"Cheers." The phone went dead.

She dropped her head against the wall with a thud.

How am I going to manage the next two weeks? Oh, crap, what if it takes longer? And what if his wife-to-be finds out about us? What if Eva's right, and she'll be a narcissistic bitch? I wonder how long I can last until Devlin finds a replacement for me? At least I don't have to fear his fiancée's fangs.

***

Three days after her call to Devlin, Rebecca stood on the pier in the early morning light. She pulled the pins from her long platinum hair and it fell over her shoulders as it did every morning since they arrived. The autumn breeze caught the long strands as she opened her robe, letting it fall about her ankles. The brisk air surrounded her bare skin as she turned from the house and garage.

Rebecca heard a car roll onto the cobblestone behind her. And she knew Devlin had arrived by the sound of the car door. She didn't bother to turn, afraid to see him. This was her time before the craziness of everything would fall on her shoulders. The grief seemed to paralyze the staff, and she had to be on her toes more than ever.

Taking a deep breath, she dove beneath the steaming surface of the dark waters. That instant, vexing cold surrounded her. Swimming from the dock, she found her rhythm as her mind cleared, and this was her form of meditation.

Later, to avoid the initial greeting with Devlin, Rebecca took longer to prepare after her swim and found some annoying chores she had put off. But eventually the call came, Rebecca had to face

by K.A. Monaco

him, the first time in four years.

Chapter 20

Facing Devlin

Standing at the door of the study, she knocked and dreaded this moment. When Devlin replied, she opened the door slightly enough to poke her head in the gap. But she had settled within herself that she wouldn't make this easy for him.

"You called for me, sir?" Rebecca asked.

"Yes," Devlin replied. "Come in."

Rebecca hesitated, then stepped back from the door and took a moment to regroup her thoughts, hoping the anxiety would lessen. It didn't. She entered and crossed much of the room, stopping about mid-way.

She liked this library, a large room filled with soft leather seats, a new selection of books, side tables, and a beautiful mahogany desk. A seat had been built beneath one of the windows and took in the view of the lake. It became her favorite spot. All the furniture came with the house, and Rebecca didn't see the need to improve the modern décor. It was a sharp contrast to the Victorian style of the old manor.

Devlin sat at the desk, and she studied him as he tarried. His messy hair had been cut shorter than the last time she saw him. He wore his charcoal gray Brioni suit but it appeared uncharacteristically rumpled. His tie lay loose around his neck. Still handsome, his face hadn't changed over the years of his absence. His cologne lingered in the air between them. It brought back bitter sweet memories.

A brandy sat near his open briefcase, and paperwork fanned across his desk in chaotic array. He slouched, and rested his head upon his hand, as if a weight pressed him down. He focused briefly on one paper, then shifted to another, and finally drifting to stare into space, only to snap himself out of it again. He deeply sighed repeatedly in only a few moments. He scooped up some papers while straightening the stragglers. In the process, his briefcase fell shut and he hastened to reopen it, almost toppling his brandy on the floor. Nothing about Devlin's actions reflected the suave, in-charge man of industry she knew several years before. She attributed this to his hectic schedule, impending wedding, and grief.

"Closer," he muttered. She took a giant step and stopped.

"Do you need a formal invitation?" he said, gruffly. "*Come here.*"

Rebecca crept forward until she could touch the leather-trimmed desktop. Rising to attention, she scanned the room for anything to place her focus on other than him. A large painting of a mid-nineteenth-century hunting party on horseback with a slew of beagles hung from the wall behind him. Regarding the painting, she gained a bit of pride, thinking of her accomplishments.

"Sit," he growled with his head down.

"No," she replied. "I prefer to stand."

Devlin shook his head with a rough groan, and continued to scribble his signature. Placing that document aside, he pulled another before him.

"I didn't see you this morning at the greeting," he said, then signed his name again.

"That's correct."

"You had something *more* important to do, I presume?"

"Technically—I'm not required to be on duty until 8 am. What I do before 8 is my business."

"When I'm not in residence." He sipped his brandy. "That is correct." He continued to scan the next document. "But on the days I'm expected, or already here, my staff is to be present at any meeting I desire. This property has become laxed where the rules are concerned."

Rebecca could tell by the way he avoided looking at her that he used his paperwork as a shield. She scoffed. "How would you know? You haven't been here. You've distanced yourself from this manor like we had leprosy." She regretted her words and knew she over stepped her rank in the house. "I apologize. I shouldn't have said that."

Devlin's eyes remained downcast as he sat still. She wondered if she angered him with her bluntness. But his silence infuriated her. The pain that she had brushed aside and tried to ignored flared hot. She couldn't suppress her hurt and anger any longer.

She snapped the necklace from her neck that he had given her and tossed it on the pile of papers. Before he moved, she slapped her cell phone on the desk, then shut the laptop that sat on the edge and tossed it before him. Slowly, he picked up the fine, gold chain in his fingers and stared at it, as if contemplating its purchase.

"Congratulations, Lord Englewood. You succeeded where an up-and-coming gangster failed, to make me feel like a two-bit whore."

She felt relieved of the anger, but only momentarily. She had rehearsed so much more in the mirror over the time of their absence, but what she said satisfied her for now. Turning on her heels, she strutted for the door then heard his chair move and slowed. The confrontation wouldn't be over that easily.

"Wait," Devlin's said in a placid tone. "Wasn't there a fourth item I gave you?"

She stopped mid-room, faced him to see he had pushed his seat back and folded his hands in his lap. The absence of emotion in his face annoyed her but he continued to stare at the desk top.

"Gave?" she questioned. "More like paid for services rendered. Yes, I burned that dress years ago."

"If I disrespected you so, why have you stayed? You could've left at any time during my absence."

"You told Madam Eva that no one leaves your employment alive."

"You were eavesdropping? That was a private conversation."

"There was no such thing as privacy in the old house. And where would I have gone? Nearly a hundred years since my family left New York, with no education, or means to live on, not even a social security number."

Devlin held up a paper that had rested at the corner of his desk. She recognized her request for transfer letter that dangled from his fingers. Again, his eyes wouldn't meet hers.

"You didn't think I'd protest this?" he asked. "You could have run away, but instead you place a formal resignation?"

"If you took the time to read it, you'd see where I acknowledge that *with* your peculiar lifestyle…" She inhaled to calm her speedy ascension into anger.

"Peculiar lifestyle?" He rose.

"… That you wouldn't be able to let me go. But I'm seeking a transfer to one of your relative's estates. Preferably somewhere you visit the least."

He glanced up, dropped the paper and rounded the desk. A quick peek at him and a shocked look covered his face. Rebecca turned away, shielding her cheek with her hand as she remembered how her appearance had changed after she fed. Nearly two months yet the residual effects lingered, radiant skin, bright eyes and well-pronounced highlights in her hair. Such a remarkable change that women stopped her on the street to compliment her.

First, he approached her from behind, then he began to circle her. Suddenly, her fear ignited and she wanted to escape.

"I'll be sure to attend the next meeting," she said abruptly.

"Will that be all?"

"No," he replied. "Look at me."

She felt flushed and weak in the knees as he inspected her. She caught his gaze more than once with his eyes wide from wonder.

"You're—more beautiful than I remember," he muttered.

"It's been years, sir. Your memory of me faded over time."

"No, I remember you quite well. Are you doing something different?"

"Yes," Rebecca replied, thinking quickly. "Change of diet and some exercise."

"Or perhaps it's the morning swims in the lake? I didn't see a bathing suit." Devlin grinned. "Not that I could see much from the driveway."

"Nothing you haven't seen already. But if it distracts you, I'll be sure to wear something, at least for the short time you're here."

"No." Devlin chuckled. "Far be it from me to tell a woman what to wear. And I'll be remaining here indefinitely."

Oh, shit.

"And a transfer is not possible. I've caught hell for having normal people in my employment. The family strictly employs Familiars, and in that my homes differ from those of my family. Placing you in one of their estates would be risky for you. And I need you here to replace the Madam."

"Many in this house have been here much longer than I. They should have had a chance at this position. My leaving would end any ill feelings."

"I don't think any of them want the job," Devlin said. "In fact, had you attended the morning greeting, you would have been surprised by the compliments the staff had concerning you in this new position. They seem content. I'd go so far as to say—happy. And that without suckling speaks volumes of your abilities."

"That's odd because most of them have blamed me for your absence. But I'm not happy here."

"Aren't you?" Devlin stood before her. "Look me in the eye and tell me these people don't mean anything to you. You've served beside them for decades. And now they're under your direct care. Could you entrust anyone else?"

Boldly, Rebecca met his gaze, but surprised herself when she couldn't confirm it. With everything in her, she wanted to leave, see new places, and work for anyone other than him. But he was correct concerning the staff. They were her family. He had let some of the wind out of her sails. She sighed, ashamed and disappointed in her lack of cold, impartiality.

Chapter 21

The New Estate

Devlin returned to his position behind the desk. When he faced her again, his countenance softened. "For what it's worth, it's good to see you." He sat. She turned, trying to focus on the equestrians in the painting. "Didn't you think I'd want to see you?"

"More like, I—didn't want to see you. I placed all matters that concerned you upon your desk before your arrival. I assumed you'd attend to them in your prompt and efficient manner. I typed up your itinerary and a small speech for the viewing."

"Yes, I saw that. Quite fitting and she would have liked it."

"I laid out a gray suit, since your black suits, you think, make you look too pale. The viewing is at six. We need to be on the road by five. The funeral is at ten tomorrow morning. What do we have to discuss?"

"Perhaps the new house? My manor in the city in which we are not standing in? A Range Rover parked in a driveway attached to a house I don't remember purchasing. My Phantom Rolls and its demise, just to name a few."

"Didn't Eva explain all this in your last conversation with

her?"

"No," Devlin said. "That conversation never came around to this. I have to say, it was a shock when Carmichael didn't pull into the manor. I totally missed going through the tunnels. When the countryside began to flash in the windows, I questioned him. But he remained tight-lipped. Why and how…?"

"Well, with the increased crime in New York City, Eva desired to keep us safe. One of the women on staff had almost been raped. A bizarre serial killer began killing people just across the street in Central Park, that went on for almost two years. The Phantom had been totaled in a carjacking. And despite the six-foot, chain-link fence we installed around the back of the house, the homeless scaled it to enjoy our garbage. We looked into security systems and cameras, but everything utilized the cloud. Your— situation made cloud technology not a suitable resource. I think it gave her peace knowing we'd be safer in the country."

"I appreciate the sensitivity to my privacy."

"Madam Eva found out from the servants of your uncles, that it was customary to have a new house when their master acquired another mistress or, in your case, a wife. The purchase of this house rectified both situations."

"My wife?" Devlin let out a chuckle. "What about my special diet?"

"That was one of the many reasons this house stood out to us. There are two correctional facilities less than fifty miles from here. The new dungeon is in the rear of the garage. I tried to simulate the

Manhattan house's design as much as possible. I told the contractor that we liked to stage medieval dinner parties."

"And he believed you?"

"Yes. He said he had many clients with excentric tastes. The grounds had some outbuildings we renovated for the servant's quarters and a subterranean tunnel connects it to the house. There was only a modest two-bay garage when we found it."

"How did you convince the bank to allow you to construct when I have yet to go through settlement?"

"They were motivated sellers. And your reputation proceeds you. Seemed they really wanted your business."

"Why so motivated?" he asked suspiciously.

"A horrific multi-murder took place on the premises about six years ago. You know, full disclosure and all. I figured that would matter little to you. It was a short sale because the bank couldn't move it. The last walk-thru was over three years ago. So, I negotiated 200K off the original asking price with a stipulation that we were allowed to improve the land outside of contract. Should you refuse to take possession, we would forfeit all improvements and owe the costs out of pocket."

"Short sale?" he gasped. "Full disclosure, and 200K off? God, I love it when you talk dirty. How much is this setting me back?"

"It doesn't cost any more than the Manhattan house to maintain, in fact, less. The prime rate was only at five and a half percent. The rent covers everything here and is what we used for the initial down payment for the contractors. The rest of the construction costs will be rolled into the mortgage."

"Did you say rent?"

"You still own the house in Manhattan." Rebecca pointed to the lease agreement folded on top of his desk. "You're subletting it to a pharmaceutical company for their out-of-town executives, and they were thrilled to have such an elegant facility fully furnished. Now the rent we receive from that pays the mortgage here. In fact, you get paid separately for the rental of the furnishings and we took out insurance in case anything is damaged, of which they pay. With the housing market still in a slump, I couldn't get my asking price, so I didn't sell. I heard real estate is all about timing."

"Keep talking, I'm getting turned on. How did you afford the jet? You didn't purchase that as well?"

"No, having negotiated with one of the owners of the pharmaceutical company, he insisted I utilize their jet if I pay for the fuel and pilot's salary. It cost slightly more than your tickets for two people to fly first class and with your fiancé's, perhaps, sensitive condition after being changed, you'd need the privacy."

"As always, your thoughtfulness astounds me."

"I see she didn't come with you."

"No, she remained in Paris. I take it this is all your doing."

"Someone had to take over when you left us for so long. Eva wasn't equipped for you to just abandon us. And even she admitted she couldn't adjust to modern life. She still used ledger paper to record transactions and balance the books. Soon after I started college, I took that over, and made it look more like a balance sheet for your convenience."

"Yes, I noticed, and I like all your improvements. I'm impressed."

"I didn't do it to impress you. But someone had to step up and take care of everyone."

"College has changed you, or didn't I see this—ambitious, cut-throat side of you before? I have to tell you; it makes you even more attractive."

Don't say anything about throats.

She ignored his comment with an eye roll. "I think I've always been ambitious, but college showed me how to master it. My shooting merely slowed me down for a bit. Do you think I would wait idly for you all these years?"

"I don't know what I thought. I avoided thinking about you because it hurt. I missed you terribly." He paused and glanced at her. "And you're so beautiful. I can't get over how…"

"Tomorrow," Rebecca interrupted. "You're expected to sign some papers concerning Eva after the funeral, and the bank requires settlement the day after. The bank insisted on your soonest availability when they found out you'd be in town next. And I figured you'd be heading back to Europe soon after the funeral so I arranged the meeting."

"So soon?"

"I don't want open issues for a new house manager to inherit. And you can't blame the bank; they graciously allowed us to renovate and construct before closing. It's nice doing business with your reputation. When will your fiancé be joining you here?"

Devlin didn't answer while staring at her which made her feel even more uneasy.

A knock at the door and Elizabeth poked her head in. "Mistress? The vans are here. The drivers ask for you to sign the rental agreement and I know you said about inspecting them before you signed."

"Yes, I'll be there in a moment." The door closed. "I have to go. If you have any other questions. I'll be around."

Devlin rose as she neared the door. "I'm sorry I wasn't here for Eva. But I had no clue. She never told me she was sick, not even on her last phone call. But I could hear it in her voice. I thought I had more time. She always told me not to worry, that she'd be fine. Do you know why she wouldn't have told me?"

"I think she wanted to die. Maybe she feared you'd suckle and she would cheat death again."

"Perhaps."

"I—would have called but I thought she explained everything before she passed."

"That may have been her intent. I take it she didn't inform you of that conversation?"

"Not a word," Rebecca said. "And it's none of my business. Please, sir. Consider my transfer seriously. I don't want friction between me and your new wife. I think it would be better for all if I found another place to work. Now you need to prepare for the viewing. Oh, and are you in need of your delivery expedited?

"No, I had a bite on the way here. If you know what I mean."

"I do." *And how I could tear open a jugular right about now.*

"One more thing?" Devlin asked, reluctantly. "May I ask a favor of you? I don't know why, but I'm feeling at such a loss. Normally, I can shift from business to personal things without hesitation, or deal with multiple financial transactions like most people order lunch. But I'm sensing Eva's loss more than I expected. I feel lost. She took care of so many small and seemingly insignificant things. I wouldn't know where to start. Like you laid out my suit today, that was something she would have done. If you would—fill her shoes, just for a few days 'til all the business is concluded. I'd be very grateful. I can only imagine how you're feeling about me and I'm asking you to set your personal feelings aside to work with me."

"Really? You didn't get the impression that I'm a little hurt?"

"Yes, but…"

"I'll be at your disposal—for a time. But I'll only help you to the extent that Madam Eva would have. Don't think our past gives you special privileges."

"Of course, I wouldn't think of taking advantage, knowing our history."

Rebecca nodded, not able to stand another moment in his presence. Once on the other side, she caught herself about to buckle at the knees. Crying, she felt waves of frustration and pain pour out of her. Heading for the garage, she removed her tears, welcoming the distraction when she found Carmichael and the drivers of the rental vans.

Chapter 22

The Ride to the City

At four thirty, the staff assembled in the driveway about to board the two Nissan passenger vans Rebecca had rented to drive them to the viewing. She had to borrow a nice dress from one of the women, having nothing black in her collection of hand-me-downs.

Rebecca opened the van's front door when Devlin appeared in the gray suit she had laid out for him. Carmichael pulled the Range Rover from the garage. Devlin made his way to it, then called to her.

"Mistress Rebecca, please ride with me." Devlin said in a serious tone. "We have further business to discuss."

Dreading more time alone with him, she complied seeing how Eva had left so much go unsaid. Elizabeth and Gretta, both gave her questioning looks as she grimaced. But she nodded and waved them on. She felt embarrassed and knew the staff would talk about this all the way to the funeral home.

Carmichael held the door for them then shuffled back to the driver's seat. She watched the gray vans take the lead as Carmichael followed behind them on the long driveway out to the main road.

Soon after, Devlin closed the window between the front and the back seats.

"What is so important that we couldn't discuss after the funeral tomorrow?"

"Tell me what happened to the Rolls?" Devlin asked, "Since you were the last one to see it whole."

"They shoved me out of the car two or three blocks away from Carmichael. Shortly after they left me, I heard a huge crash. By the time I arrived, the car was engulfed in flames."

The thought of her first feeding started her hunger again. She did what she could to conceal her drooling.

"That is not the story Carmichael told me. He said you weren't with him. That the car had been stolen while he helped you shop." Devlin's face grew in concern. "But you were with them alone? Did they hurt you? They didn't take liberties, did they?"

"No, they didn't. I wasn't hurt, just frightened. And I asked him to tell you that because I didn't want anyone to worry. I can take care of myself."

"You see, this is why my family doesn't employ anything but Familiars. It's very hard for them to lie to their masters. But I can imagine how terrified you must have been. I'm sorry. I can see why you don't want to talk about it or be in the city." Devlin fell silent for only a moment. "You asked me to find you another position. But I can't risk you not being in my employment."

"I understand. But what about working in one of your businesses?"

"I don't know of any that I could start you in, and you know too much to be let loose. I wanted to talk to you about the new property," Devlin said. "The house is—stylish, perhaps not in line with my prior tastes."

"You don't like it?" she asked.

"Let's say, it's growing on me," Devlin said. "Did the new house have anything to do with—us?"

"There was never an *us*," she growled.

"Sorry, I presumed we had a—relationship."

"…That didn't last longer than a week," she protested. "You have a strange interpretation of the word *relationship*."

"How would you define it?"

"Mutual Gratification."

"No, you felt for me—you were in love with me. That's why you stayed."

"I got over it. And I stayed for the reasons I already explained."

"I didn't walk away willingly. Business delayed my return—at first."

"More like you ran away. Did I scare you off? I seem to recall it was your idea to take it slow. Then you admitted you weren't sure you could. I was fine with you leaving, I had no expectations in the beginning. But you kept dangling the hook, raising my hopes. Finally, I moved on."

I graduated college and made something of myself.

"Yes, I heard about you and Carmichael."

"Carmichael?" Rebecca gasped. "What have you heard?"

"Eva mentioned about a year ago that you and he were an item," Devlin said.

"A date and some fooling around in the back of the car doesn't make a relationship any more than what we had."

"Why didn't things work out between you?" Devlin nodded toward the front seat.

"I couldn't stomach how he looked at me from the beginning; like I was his favorite flavor. I tried to ignore it since we came from the same era. But I can't."

"I'll admit," Devlin whispered. "Madam Eva made it sound like a lengthy relationship. It was the reason I began dating again. Even now the thoughts of it makes me jealous."

"Your jealousy is none of my concern," Rebecca said.

"Do you regret being with me?" Devlin slid closer.

"Do you really want to open this subject up for scrutiny, now?"

"If it clears the air between us, then yes."

"I was hurt, then I grew angry and now I'm bitter. My fault in all this is that I allowed myself to hope with each promise of your return. Instead, some trinket to purchase my forgiveness for your tardiness. But I did suffer. In the old manor, I couldn't escape you, even when you weren't there. Every shadow held a memory. I was expected to do my job—for you. So yes, in some ways the new house was about us."

"I'm sorry."

"You owe that apology to everyone in this household, not to me. I read into our time together thinking you cared more for me than you truly did. That was my mistake."

"Wait a minute. I did care deeply for you."

She ignored his reply. "They didn't deserve you abandoning them. They relied upon your suckling and now they're aging faster than before. I don't know about your other European households, but our lives are pretty isolated here. We don't have many associates outside of the house because of the secrets we hold. We may squabble amongst ourselves, a romance may blossom, or we have a fling. But at the end of the day, we're all we have. The staff live to serve you. You come and go. You don't see it, and not that you should. But our brief relationship affected the entire house and I had to face them when you didn't return. For a long time, they blamed me, and I blamed myself for it. If I hadn't opened the door to that affair, they'd be better off."

"So, you do regret it?"

"No. Not for one moment," Rebecca's hard demeanor melted slightly. "For the first time in decades, I felt alive. But I clung to the scraps you left behind; pain and rejection. That's what turned me bitter."

"You're not the only one that suffered during that time," Devlin muttered.

"That's right. Madam Eva began her decline about a year after you left. I slowly watched a strong, vibrant woman decay into sickness."

"That's not what I meant."

Rebecca's anger manifested in her voice rising an octave. "You have no right to claim suffering because you could've changed it at any moment. You couldn't even bother to check on her or us over the last three years. The doctors marveled at how she withstood the cancer for so long, but I knew. Your suckling did it. She'd still be alive today if you had been here. So, in a way, I killed her because I allowed myself to love you."

Rebecca felt indignant about Eva, but the grief resurfaced as she remembered Eva's last moments. She emotionally crumbled; her hands covered her face, and she wept. Devlin tried to pull her into his arms but she resisted, pulling her handkerchief. Devlin sat back in his seat and she knew he felt her rejection.

"Maybe if you explained why you didn't return," she snapped. "I wouldn't be so hurt. I didn't expect you to fall in love with me after all those years. I even warned you that I wasn't the same girl you fell in love with."

"I didn't return because of the way you reacted to the Crumbs. You were disgusted with how I feed," Devlin said, diverting his eyes as his expression changed to shame. "And you should be. I couldn't chase the remembrance of the look on your face in the dungeon that night. Everyone under my roof should be repulsed that I feed on your kind. It's so brutal, yet it is what it is. And I'm a despised creature and rightly so. I can't change that." Devlin paused. "My family warned me about turning someone like you. Fasting while you detest what you have become then binging as your survival instincts take over. You'd be in a constant cycle that would eventually make you regret your change. At that time, I couldn't see a future for us then if I couldn't change you. Most of the women I've married embrace the lifestyle—seeing the attributes; their vanity of never aging, living forever, endless wealth, and travel. But not you. You loved me…"

Rebecca was about to object.

"… and don't try to lie, you did love me," he said. "For all the right reasons, but I couldn't turn you into this."

"Why didn't you tell me this?" she asked. Her heart leaped into her throat. She suppressed a smile and tightened her lips, while her ears still felt the fire from her anger.

"Because if I saw you," Devlin faltered. "I wouldn't have been able to leave you again. All I wanted was to be with you."

"Well, all of this doesn't matter because you're getting married to someone else. But I thank you for finally explaining this and for closure."

"Not anymore. I called off the wedding a while ago. But I didn't have a chance to tell Eva before last week. I thought she would have told you."

"What did Eva say to you that made you change your mind?" Rebecca asked suspiciously. She feared Eva had told him of her unsettled state or that she had changed into his kind.

"She called me an idiot and how bitter you had become. I knew I was to blame. And your bitterness proves that I was right, you had feelings deeper than I gave you credit for. Then she told me the affair with him had been over for a while. And that you still loved me. I realized I made so many mistakes. I ran from the only person who ever accepted me for who and what I am. Once I realized it, I broke the engagement. I'm still madly in love with you. I dated, but it was only so I'd stop thinking about you, which never worked. I couldn't stop. My family pressured me to announce my engagement more to establish normalcy again. They think a wife would settle me down. Truly, I didn't think I hurt you so badly. If it is any conciliation, I asked Eva all the time about you. She lied and said you were fine. I thought you were—uncaring and that it meant little to you."

"If you broke up months ago, why did you wait to return until now?"

"I needed to arrange things in London so that I could return here with every intention of courting you properly. I was about to set my plans to return when you called."

"Why would you think I would want you back? You broke my heart with that other woman." Rebecca paused. "Is she still alive?"

"Yes, I jilted her, but she deserved it. I knew she was only after my money."

"You didn't change her—to be one of your kind yet?"

"No." Devlin drew closer. "She didn't know that I was a *kind*. And if I could be with her having not changed her, I realized I could do the same with you."

"Eleven months engaged—and she never suspected anything?

How stupid was she?"

"I'll admit, it wasn't her brains I was interested in."

"And you never told her what was coming? Would you have told her or just changed her without giving her a choice?"

Like you did me? Was I even an accident?

"Of course, I would have told her before the wedding," Devlin said. "This is the hardest part of my life, testing a woman's loyalty before I risk telling her what I am. Exposing who I am requires me to endure her horror and possibly her rejection, at which point I must retain my secret through the forfeiture of her life."

Devlin's eyes dropped and she detected shame in them. He sat back and folded his hands together before his face. A posture she had seen him in when he focused intensely.

"Maybe, subconsciously," Devlin said. "I don't pick mates of good character in recent years for the fear of truly falling in love with them. If they reject me over this, I have to kill them. I pick a mate that I don't connect with in case I have to terminate their life. But finding one who accepts me is only the beginning. She would have to survive the changing process. And if she died, I'd grieve as well."

"How many have you killed?" Rebecca asked, fearing his response.

"Five or six," he replied sadly. "But it dawned on me then that you already know my secret. And if you don't want to change, it doesn't mean we can't be together."

"Well, that situation hasn't changed for me, if anything—it's worse. I don't know…"

"You don't want to be with me because you don't love me anymore or you can't because of what I feed on disgusts you?" he asked.

Rebecca had a hundred thoughts and feelings running through her as he spoke. Her anger dwindled quickly and confusion set in.

Just because he repented doesn't mean I can let him hurt me again. Eva had been right; vampires were fickle. "If you loved me *so much*," she said, sarcastically, "why didn't you recognize me when we met again?"

"You changed, physically," Devlin said. "How was I to know you didn't dye when Roberts said you did? Then I thought he killed you. Your hair turned white, your eyes darkened, and you seemed taller than the little Rebecca I remembered. How was I to know it was you? But it was the tango that brought it all back to me. You're the first woman I fell in love with her soul. Your body, for most men was attractive, but I've had women with—well, bodies the devil would sell his own soul to be with for a night. But the way you looked at me after we danced. Like there was nothing I could keep hidden from you."

"And now I'm supposed to just fall in to your arms like nothing ever happened? I'm not a fool anymore, Devlin."

"Can't you forgive me, or maybe we can start over?"

"Too much as happened to start over," Rebecca said. "I've already forgiven you, but broken trust isn't something one can just forget. It's tainted everything you've touched."

He sighed with frustration then rallied. "I'll wait. Be it four years or forty. I'll show you I can be trusted."

"I don't know, that would require you not to lie. I don't think you're capable of that." The nasty quip surprised her.

"Ouch," Devlin said.

"I can't do this now." Rebecca felt emotional and confused. "We have the viewing in only a few moments and the funeral tomorrow. I can't see beyond that. And I changed over the last few years—in ways…"

"I understand. You need time to think, but know that I want to spend the rest of *your life with you,* however long that is. I feel a connection I never felt with anyone else. Even if it takes your lifetime, I want to make it up to you." Devlin rested his hand on her arm. She pulled away as if his touch were toxic. Closing her eyes, she stifled her tears and moved toward the door. She only wanted to escape.

"But if you truly don't have feelings for me anymore, or it is too painful..." Devlin slid back against the door on his side of the car with his shoulders slumped. "I'll see what I can do to transfer you. I don't want to cause you anymore pain."

"That is decent of you." Rebecca felt conflicted, her heart tearing into two.

Her anger and inner strength were crumbling like a brick wall after a wrecking ball. He said all the right words to win her back, but trust was earned, not given. Could she trust him and herself to allow love to spring up again?

She diverted her eyes to the floor and kept them there. Once the SUV parked at the funeral home, she dashed to the restroom but even there she had no privacy for a good cry.

Chapter 23

Saying Goodbye

The funeral home felt depressing, and Rebecca knew it would be a stressful afternoon even before Devlin brought up their past. She and Devlin were first in the line to see Madam Eva in the casket. The staff hesitated and loitered among the chairs. Devlin remarked about her smile. She knew that permanently frozen grin had been there since she suckled. But something was off.

"This isn't the coffin Eva chose," Rebecca said, noticing the upgraded silver handles and plush silk lining.

"I called the funeral home from the plane and changed it," Devlin whispered, looking into the coffin with sad eyes. "She gave to everyone, cared for us so well, yet was so frugal with her own needs. She never allowed me to show her my appreciation. Now she can't argue with me about this. I'm glad she's wearing the gown she wore to the Crumbs. It was her favorite and always made her look so elegant. I just wish I could have been there for her last moments, to tell her what she meant to me, that she was like family."

Devlin's voice grew weak. He excused himself, and Rebecca followed him. He stood with his back to the others, bowing his head, and squeezed his eyes to keep from crying. Rebecca pulled out his handkerchief from his breast pocket and offered it to him. He wiped the tears that wouldn't stop falling.

"I know men aren't supposed to cry," he said.

"It's alright," Rebecca grabbed his arm. She felt herself beginning to tear. "We'll miss her terribly. I'm no substitute for her."

"She had more experience," Devlin said. "But don't sell yourself short. Given the time she had, you'd be even better. If I didn't say anything before, thank you for taking care of this."

"She was my friend," Rebecca said sympathetically. "It was my pleasure to help her."

A deep, mournful sigh arose from Devlin. His depth of sadness surprised her. Eva was only his house manager, but she had been with him for over two centuries. Rebecca had lived day in and day out with Eva, assuming the relationship to be deeper than his. But she was wrong. Eva had done more for both of them with little recognition.

Devlin recovered and put on a brave face as he returned to the casket. Rebecca stood close, and he wouldn't let her leave his side for the rest of the night. They shook hands with the staff, and some of those Madam Eva had professional relations with throughout the current decade. Even the black man they met under the bridge made an appearance.

Looking into the staff's eyes as they formed a line at the funeral home, they looked as lost as she felt. They milled around for two hours in their respective groups, reminiscing, weeping, and telling tales about Madam Eva. By eight they returned to the vans for departure. Many remarked that the Crumbs wouldn't be the same without her.

For Devlin, small talk and business filled the ride back to the new estate. He answered several phone calls from the West Coast. With the interior light over Devlin, the glare hindered her from watching the countryside through her window. Instead, she surfed her phone, watching cat reels trying to lighten her sad heart.

But when Devlin took a call from his broker in town, something sparked her interest. As they spoke, she pulled up the stock exchange on her phone. She had delved a little with her education. But much of the lingo still sounded like Greek to her. About to abort the effort, she saw something that piqued her interest.

"I'm sorry to be doing business on your time, but the viewing took a while," Devlin said. "Yes, thank you for your patience." Devlin listened, then replied. "No, sell that stock and buy more Goldman Sachs for now."

"Why are you so stuck on Dow Jones?" Rebecca muttered softly. "Glarmin on the S&P 500 had a 28% return in three months." She focused on her phone as she scrolled over more stocks. "Horrid year for Sachs," she muttered, still very low.

Devlin held his hand over the microphone. "What was that?"

"Nothing," she replied.

"No, what did you say about the S&P?"

"Just that Glarmin had a good return over the last three months," Rebecca said. "And their perspective is solid. Should show continual growth in the future. See. I had to write a short paper on them for school."

She held the phone up for him as she enlarged the screen. Devlin quickly scrutinized the information, which surprised her. She didn't claim to understand all the numbers and symbols, but it seemed as if he did; like some kind of savant.

"Change that," Devlin told the broker. "Purchase 18 shares of Glarmin and let it ride for a few months. We'll revisit this in December. Yes, that's all. Good night."

He actually listened to me?

Devlin turned toward her, his mouth open when his phone buzzed again. He took the call and held up his finger as if she should wait for him. But the calls were endless and took up the entire trip home. She didn't envy his fast-paced world but felt gratified that he listened.

***

Devlin's evening meal tempted Rebecca, but she refrained. She knew she couldn't hide what she had become much longer. But finding the words to broach the subject grew even harder. And though he said he loved her and wanted to marry her, would he have to kill her if his family rejected his choice?

Rebecca's role as acting Madam gave her every excuse to avoid what happened in the dungeon. And Devlin didn't suspect that her aversion to blood had changed. Making the final arrangements for the wake with a caterer in town in person, Rebecca hesitated to return, but Carmichael pressed her to hurry. He didn't want to miss the evening's event. Even with the Crumbs, the staff remained in mourning.

When she arrived back at the house, she smelled the blood emanating from the dungeon as she exited the garage. Whether it was only the thought or the actual scent, her stomach groaned. Hurrying to her room, she allowed herself a few sips from a blood bag to curb her appetite. But the rationing grew difficult to maintain and her desire to consume the entire bag more tempting.

***

The next day, as the grave-side service concluded, rain started to pelt the freshly dug ground at the gravesite. After a brief ceremony, the casket was lowered into the ground. Black umbrellas sprouted like morning glories around Rebecca as others took shelter under them. One of the funeral directors held his umbrella for her. She felt the loss much more than she had thought she would.

Rebecca didn't need to see Devlin to know he hovered close by. The slight sound of his phone vibrated in his pocket. He was never very far and handsome in his dark gray suit. During the ceremony, he touched her back or arm to comfort her and showed kindness to everyone. Though she wanted, desperately to stay angry with him, she couldn't.

Everyone took their turn tossing a handful of dirt on the lowered coffin, but Rebecca felt frozen in her spot. Eva's guidance over the years had provided her comfort and purpose. She had trained to take over as the house manager, but on the eve of doing so, wanted more. She wanted a life. Though not a Familiar, Eva seemed satisfied serving Devlin's kind and she marveled at it.

Most of the house staff had started to head for the van. Hesitating, she felt Devlin touch her arm. But not until he stood between her and the grave did she focus on anything else. He didn't have to say anything. His eyes held the sympathy she needed. She crumbled, leaning against his chest. His arms rose to hold her and they felt strong. Where he seemed weak the night before, now it was her turn. After a moment, he pulled her away.

"The Eva we all loved is not in that coffin, love," Devlin whispered.

They walked to the limo while everyone from the estate piled back into the vans. When the limo driver closed the door, the vans moved out. Rebecca looked back at the grave, feeling like some part of her she left behind. She had cried all the tears she could, but the ache remained.

They returned to the funeral home, where Carmichael met them in the Range Rover. The rest of the household returned to the new estate for the wake directly from the cemetery. But Rebecca and Devlin were delayed by business. She didn't mind. The new manor felt incomplete with the old Madam missing from the staff.

Rebecca strapped herself into the passenger-side back seat of the Range Rover while Devlin tended to the business at the funeral home. Carmichael retreated to the driver's seat, waiting for his master to appear. The rainwater rushed down the window, making a Monet of the scenery. She wiped a tear away.

"Are you alright, Becca?" Carmichael asked with an air of

familiarity. His concerned voice broke her aimless fixation on nothing.

"Pardon?" She glared at his reflection in the rearview mirror. Compassionate filled eyes looked back at her and his voice reflected an inappropriate relationship for their respective stations.

"I'm sorry, Mistress Bellows," Carmichael said. "Are you alright? You're not yourself."

"I'll be fine," she replied.

Rebecca turned toward the window again and used her handkerchief to blot the tears. She wanted to be quiet and wished she was alone in her room.

"Please, Mistress." Carmichael turned his body to face her through the dividing window. "Let me serve you. I'll do anything you ask. Anything, just name it. I can be anything you want."

"That is quite enough," Rebecca snapped. "Thank you for your continued offer, but I'm in no need of sex."

"I don't mean just sex. Re-assign me to be your servant, to serve you only."

"Have you gone crazy? Servants don't have servants. Speak nothing of this again, ever."

"As you wish, Mistress." Carmichael turned back around, but the way he hissed his reply hinted at something that went beyond lust, like an odd obedience or perhaps obsession.

The rear door on the driver's side opened, Devlin slid in.

"Sorry, sir," Carmichael said. "I was—preoccupied with something."

"Quite alright," Devlin said with a smile. "This is not the weather I'd expect you to wait outside for me."

Carmichael drove out of the lot. Devlin focused on his phone as Rebecca watched the buildings flash by, or nothing at all.

Chapter 24

Bad Timing

The black SUV pulled out of the funeral home and headed through the busy streets of Manhattan just before noon. Traffic thickened, and their progress slowed to a crawl. Umbrellas of all colors covered the crowded sidewalks. Lost in thought, Rebecca watched the city when Devlin drew her attention by closing the dividing window.

"I don't like the way he looks at you," Devlin muttered. "I never noticed it before."

"That started only recently—after the carjacking," Rebecca replied. "He's overly concerned with my welfare, which is another reason to find another place to work. Don't concern yourself about it."

"It is my concern," Devlin turned to her. "I returned early because of the funeral, but I was on my way back to you, and I intend to stay this time."

"London or Europe isn't going to yank your chain?" she asked bitterly. "One call from them and you'd be gone again?"

"Are you insinuating that my family manipulated to keep us apart?"

"How would I know if they did or didn't? I know Milan

didn't seem important, then you never showed up. You were to return for the weekend, and you had flown somewhere else. Then it happened again and again. And finally, you vanished like a bad dream. And all of us suffered then."

Rebecca noticed the rain had stopped, and the sun broke through the clouds, warming the window. She would have liked to bask in the sunlight and the silence, but Devlin persisted.

"Do you know why I procrastinated my wedding for eleven months?" Devlin asked. "Because of you."

"Don't blame me for your problems," Rebecca said sharply. "I didn't sabotage your engagement. I could have contacted your fiancé and made a real mess of things for you. But I took the high road and let you be. And again—none of my concern." Rebecca turned away to watch the scenery, hoping the conversation would drop. "I'm just part of your staff."

"Bloody bullshit," Devlin exploded. "You've always meant more to me than that. You don't believe me, now. I procrastinated because I couldn't stop thinking about you or us. There hasn't been a week or even a day that I didn't regret walking away from you. I thought if I kept away, you'd be better off. But I can't. I've missed you and I was a loon for letting it go on this long."

"And you could have called me. I carried this phone with me all the time."

"Countless times I almost dialed you. You could have called me, too."

"Forgive me," Rebecca snapped. "I'm a little old-fashioned.

A woman doesn't call a man unless she wants to be considered a floozy."

"And sleeping with me after our first date didn't do that?" Devlin stopped. He grimaced as he realized his words. "I'm sorry. I didn't mean it."

"You should be sorry. And I just didn't hop in bed with you, I waited almost eighty years to make love to you. And it was love, not sex. But I wasn't the one who left. I kept waiting. *I* was stupid. Why are you doing this now? Isn't it hard enough with Eva's death? What do you want from me?"

She turned back to the window as the city high-rises slowly drifted by. Most of the umbrellas were gone, she watched the crowd as they walked faster than the SUV. With bumper-to-bumper traffic, she longed to talk to Eva.

"I want you," Devlin said. "Because I love you."

"And your family?" she asked. "You still need to ask for their approval. And if they reject me, what then? I'm dessert?"

"We make it a practice not to feed on women or children," Devlin said.

"Besides, I'm only a servant. And if you think I'm old-fashioned, they're probably worse. Do you think they'll accept one of the staff as your new wife?"

"You're not a Familiar," Devlin said. "And I can handle them."

"You shouldn't have to." Rebecca yelled to draw Carmichael's attention. "Stop the car."

"I'll do what it takes to have you." Devlin gripped her arm, as his eyes turned greedy. "I won't live without you."

"Stop acting like a selfish child. And how long will it last this time? Let go."

"I've always wanted you."

Rebecca didn't know why, but she knew he spoke the truth. She didn't lacked love for him or want him any less than before. But what she needed was time alone to sort out her feelings. Rebecca pulled from his grasp, opened the door, and leaped out of the car.

Devlin followed. "Am I a fool, Rebecca?" He stopped outside the door of the SUV.

She stalled in her steps when he said it.

"Did you ever love me?" he asked, his voice sincere and insecure.

"You're such an idiot," Rebecca turned to face him as tears streamed down her face. "From the beginning, I've loved you. And even now, and probably without end. Even the monster that hides inside of you couldn't deter me. But you didn't even allow me to react one way or another. *You—left—me.*"

"Becca, Mistress Bellows," Carmichael appeared around the corner. "You should get back in the car. I'll leave the master here if you want me to."

"Carmichael?" Devlin said. "You work for me. Now bugger off."

"You're upsetting her," Carmichael replied.

"We're discussing something that is none of your business."

Devlin glared at him.

"I won't have you disrespecting her," Carmichael stood his ground.

Both men straightened their torsos as if ready for a brawl. Rebecca tasted the tangible testosterone in the confrontation.

"Just shut up, both of you," Rebecca said. "I'm not some toy to fight over and I'm so tired of being told what to do and how to feel. Now, the one person I could really use some advice from is dead. And I never thought I'd miss her this much. And no one is giving me the time to mourn. And you act like I have no choice in this. If you want to court me properly, start by asking me, not demanding."

Rebecca shook her head. "I should never have danced with you that night. No, I don't mean that. I can still see you in that long overcoat coming across the dance floor. You were handsome, and I wanted you. But nothing has worked out right. And I mean nothing. So please, I need to think alone and away from you, him, and everyone who wants something from me. I just need time to clear my head before I say or do some things I don't mean."

Surprised at her boldness, Rebecca headed for the large gated entrance to Central Park. Devlin's footfalls told her he followed.

"But, mistress, this is the park?" Carmichael warned.

She turned, still walking, and glared at him for a second. "I know where we are."

"But it's dangerous, love," Devlin said, moving toward her, but she didn't stop. "A few hours, it'll be dusk. It won't be safe."

"Don't play the chivalrous protector." Rebecca looked at her watch. "For someone with more time than anyone on this planet, why can't you give me at least a few hours alone? I'm not a yoyo, Devlin. Carmichael and every other servant in the house act like I'm some goddess. I never wanted to be worshipped, just loved. Besides, how can I trust you now?"

"Because I love you," Devlin said, spanning the gap between them. "I'll show you, but you must let me in."

"Why? So, you can hurt me again?" she asked. "No, you'll have to show me some other way. For now, go. You need to be back in the city by ten tomorrow morning to tie up loose ends at the bank. It will take you the rest of the afternoon to navigate through the traffic and tunnels. I'll meet up with you tomorrow."

"Please, love. Don't push me away. I don't want to live without you." Devlin reached out to touch her cheek, but she slapped it away.

"Maybe I'll feel differently tomorrow," Rebecca said. "I just need some space right now."

Devlin nodded and headed back to the SUV.

"Take him home, Carmichael," she yelled. "If you want to help me…"

"Yes, of course," Carmichael said. "As you wish."

Carmichael dashed to the driver's side.

What has gotten into all these men?

Rebecca paused under the wrought-iron gate's entrance to the park. Usually, she would have loved looking at the gothic dark-painted metal. It would have reminded her of the view from her bedroom in the old manor, but Devlin flustered her too much to enjoy it, even for a brief moment.

"Call, and I'll come for you," Devlin called from the open window.

"Don't worry about me; I'll find a hotel."

She walked on.

Devlin continued to protest, then grew silent, but she didn't turn to see if the SUV waited. Once within the gates, she slowed her pace. People passed her, but she stared at the walk, lost in grief and skeptical of a future with Devlin. If Eva knew Devlin had called off the wedding, why didn't she mention it? What would she have said that made him change his mind?

Two-hours passed as she wandered through the park. Passersby didn't distract her as echoes of Devlin's words revolved around her mind. Her heart craved him, urged her to let her guard down, and hoped everything would work out. Without Eva to ask, Rebecca feared trusting her judgment.

It hurts to see him, and it hurts to be without him. But if I still hurt over him, it means there is still love in me. How can I trust him? But he seems so sincere. Eva said he asked about me when he called. Had I told her how I felt earlier, would she have told him? Would things have been different?

Remaining in the shadows for all those years was my mistake. How much of my sorrow have I caused? I can't blame him for all this. I can't be a servant any longer. Not now. His family won't accept me. Who am I fooling? Only myself.

What will he think when he finds out who, I mean, what I have become? In one way, it makes things easier. But now he wants me to be what I was. I can't go back, or can I? I could ask him, but then he'd find out. I doubt I have anything to fear from him, but his family is the real threat. No unsanctioned vampires, Eva said. What should I do?

She stopped and stared at the sidewalk. *I only really have one alternative. I must choose Devlin if I want to live. I love him and choosing him isn't only to preserve my life. I would rather starve than to be like this if it was just me alone. I've loved him and always will. But will he be faithful to me?*

Our love had the strength to survive our separation. By preferring my frailties where feeding is concerned over making me like him, shows he's not selfish. He's sacrificed his happiness for me. And he didn't move on until he thought I had. But these are his words. How do I know he's not lying again. No, I know he's not lying. How do I know? Do I trust my instincts? Do I trust love?

Rebecca walked briefly when the sunset cast long shadows across the cement and walkways. She recognized the reservoir in the twilight and knew she neared the old Manhattan Manor. Part of her didn't want to see it for all the history. But it felt like home.

"I wondered how much longer I'd have to wait."

Rebecca heard a voice behind her and spun. Devlin stretched across a park bench with his arms folded under his head, as cavalier as ever. He leaped to his feet and moved to join her. Her first instinct urged her to flee, but a second thought told her it would be futile.

"What are you doing here?" Rebecca asked. "I told Carmichael to take you home."

"I don't know what's gotten into him. He defied my direct order. He wouldn't stop. I had to dive out of the car while it was still moving. There will be hell to pay when we get home."

"Take it easy on him. The whole house is going through changes. First me taking Eva's place as the new Madam, then her death, and now your return." She looked past Devlin and toward the manor. "Even I've been feeling confused lately. I mean, what was I thinking. I don't know I want to leave everyone now. I can take over Madam's place and run that house—easily. But I'm bored. Tired of being cooped up in one house or another. I was hoping the country would be different."

"Different how?"

"Different people, less pushy men. Find a place to just get a beer and hang with the house staff when they go to let off some steam. Or just a lone." Rebecca took a deep breath, then mumbled. "Devlin, there's something I need to tell you."

"First, a position as opened up recently that I think you would be very good at." Devlin said.

"Oh," Rebecca felt disappointed and nervous. "In one of the relative's houses?"

"Sort of. The position would require some travel. And you'd do similar things as now, but you'd be overseeing more people and other houses."

"Like a manager of managers?"

"Yes."

"How much does it pay?" She didn't really care but any position would be better than the one she already had. "Because I really want some clothes of my own, not these hand-me-downs."

Devlin snickered. "Absolutely nothing." She gave him a confused glare. "But you'd have access to every cent I have. And I'll buy you an entire new wardrobe."

"What kind of position is this?"

"The kind of position that you'll work very closely with me."

"A personal assistant?"

"Yes, as my wife."

"Hhhmmm." she smiled slightly at him. "I'll think about it."

"Most women wouldn't have to."

"I'm not most women, Devlin. The sooner you realize that the better your life will be."

"What do you want, Rebecca?" Devlin asked. "I'll give you anything you want. Just name it."

"No matter how I try, I just can't get past it." She turned to him. "I want you. I still love you. But I'm afraid. You don't respect me. You don't listen to me. I asked for a little time. Can't you grant me that?"

"No, I can't." Devlin smiled coyly. "I've wasted too much time already. I lied to myself that you didn't care for me like I did for you. I deceived myself into thinking I was the only one hurt in this. I'm sorry. And I'm sorry I've been a selfish, spoiled man who still needs you." Devlin gently pulled her into his arms and she let him. "But I can't take the chance of letting *you* get away from *me* this time." Devlin lifted her chin and planted his lips against hers.

Like standing at the edge of a cliff, deciding whether to jump or retreat, she leaped over the side, wrapping her arms around him. She returned his kiss with unrestrained passion. Rebecca felt happy, loved, and wanted, yet angry, vengeful, and vulnerable as the spectrum of suppressed emotions erupted like a volcano within her heart. When they parted, she slapped him hard across the face.

"Ouch," he muttered rubbing his jaw. "Where did you learn to hit like that?"

"That's for not coming back," she said. She clutched his lapel, smiled, and yanked him back against her. Pressing her soft lips against his they kissed passionately again. She felt tears of joy when they parted. He wiped them away.

"That's for saying you're sorry. But you better never be that stupid again."

"I can't guarantee that, I can be pretty stupid," Devlin said. "All I know is that I love you."

"Good, but I still don't know how to trust you. You'll have to prove yourself to me."

"How am I to prove it? Name it."

"I don't know. But I'll tell you when I'm convinced."

"Agreed."

"But you can't lie to me anymore and you must be true to your word this time."

"But when I negotiate a deal…"

"I understand in business you may need to—not be absolutely honest, *but you can't lie to me*. Just say yes."

"Yes," Devlin said.

"And…"

"I knew that wasn't the end."

"I'm no one's servant any longer. I'm your equal. You will respect me."

"Of course."

"And travel, I'm not going to be the little woman at home."

"Never," Devlin grinned. "Is that it?"

"Yes, no, I don't know. I'm figuring this out as I go along."

"Fair enough."

"Can we sit, I need a rest. It's been one hell of a day and my feet are killing me in these borrowed heels."

"Sure," Devlin said and pointed to the bench he rose from.

"No, I have a better idea." Rebecca flipped off her shoes and walked up a small knoll by the reservoir and another park bench. Then she laid in the grass, and sprawled out. "Oh, now this is lovely."

Instantly, her mind cleared of all the confusion. She bent her knees and ran her bare feet through it. Stretching, she groaned then stopped and looked thoughtfully up through the canopy of tree limbs and leaves.

"You're going to be soaked," Devlin stood over her then took a seat on the bench. "The grass is still wet."

"I do miss the old manor," Rebecca said. "Bitter sweet."

Devlin joined her in the grass and lay beside her. Rebecca pulled his arm over her and lay watching the trees above her. She didn't realize she had fallen asleep until she opened her eyes. The park's lights flickered on with the darkness.

"I fell asleep."

"Like you said. It's been a hard day for all of us."

"You should have awoke me. The police still haven't found the serial killer who was killing people here in the park."

"No, and they won't, since he moved to the country," Devlin replied.

"You know who it is?"

"It was me."

"So, you were the reason Madam moved us?"

"I lived out of hotels here in the city when I didn't return. But I couldn't stay away. I used to come here and watch you read in the window. I should have known then I couldn't live without you. Then Carmichael and I would hunt in the park. Then, after I found out you were with him. I stopped coming altogether, to punish him."

"But the murders continued after he and I…" she gasped. "Carmichael?"

Devlin nodded. "Apparently, even before he met me, he developed a taste for it. He joined the mob wanting to be a hitman. When I didn't return, he had no outlet for his passions. After the second murder in the park that I didn't do, I realized it was him and that he'd divulge my peculiar lifestyle if caught. I warned him and it stopped or he didn't get caught."

"You know, shortly after the last murder, the homeless stopped coming around."

"And their deaths usually wouldn't make the news. Carmichael has a creative way of disposing of bodies."

"I'm glad I didn't know until now."

"But it's still not safe here. And we should be going. We can find a hotel. You must be exhausted after today and this grueling week. And you haven't eaten all day."

"I'm fine. In fact, I feel—great." Rebecca stretched again. "Can we do something fun? Let's go dancing." Rebecca sat up and looked around. Devlin nodded. "And I know just the place."

Chapter 25

Craving for Crumbs

Down the street from the manor, a brick building with neon lights framed part of the structure and spelled out the word "SPARKS". She pulled Devlin by the hand as she headed for it. Outside the establishment, there was a long line of people waiting for permission to enter behind a velvet rope. She moved to take a spot at the back of the line when Devlin pulled her to the front and nodded at the doorman.

"Lord Devlin, it's been a while," the attendant said.

"Yes, it has," Devlin replied.

The man removed the chain which brought dissatisfied comments from those left outside. Rebecca mouthed a silent apology as Devlin led her past the attendant and into the building.

"That was rude," she said.

"You're entering a world where doors and lines disappear. Get used to it."

Devlin led her down a dark hallway towards a bar and dance floor. Strobes and lasers, mirrors and dry ice, everything including music so loud it made Rebecca's chest pound. Devlin wasted no time as he jumped into the sea of bodies that bounced to the rhythmic bass and percussions. With reckless abandon, Devlin made his way to the center of the dance floor and thrashed to the music like those around him. He waved for her to follow. Wading into the crowded floor, she watched the others as they moved and mimicked them.

Rebecca noticed the women spied Devlin right away. He seemed oblivious to them, caught up in the music. Her inadequacies in their rekindled relationship flared hot. And with a primal instinct to protect her man, she stepped between Devlin and the group that flirted with him. She felt the hair on the back of her neck and arms rise as her finger nails grew longer. She prepared for a fight.

Before she could snarl and reveal her fangs, Devlin pulled her around, breaking her obsession. He took her face in his hands and kissed her for all to see. Despite the loud music, she heard their disappointment.

"You don't have to worry about them, love," he whispered loudly in her ear. "I'm all yours. They won't be taking me away from you, now or ever."

When the chorus of the song came, everyone around her, including Devlin, jumped upon command. She felt the floor bouncing as they landed. Devlin's youthful, energetic ways rallied her, and she joined them. She danced harder, hoping to drain the anxiety of the day.

Nothing about Devlin revealed his age except the occasional way he spoke. He resembled those around him, spirited and free. But he wanted to court her which meant more to her than those around her would understand. At times, his eyes held a look of an old consciousness. Knowing his wisdom came from many lifetimes, she rested her mind to her anxieties of their relationship. And for the first time since Devlin left, she felt carefree and happy.

Several songs later, Rebecca felt a raging in her stomach. Then she heard it, a rhythmic tempo not made by an instrument. She smelled it, too, something that made her stomach growl as her newfound abilities intensified. The alcohol at the bar, the perfume and cologne of those around her, their sweat, and the pounding of their heartbeats accosted her senses.

At first, she thought she could suppress the urges, but they overwhelmed her. Covering her ears, she tried to control the impulses that provoked a more primitive, instinctual side of her. The hunger and lust returned like the day of the carjacking, and with her adrenaline pumping, she felt predatory. Her fingernails thickened, mouth tingled as the ends of her canines grew longer than the rest of her teeth, and salivated to the point of almost drooling.

Devlin continued dancing, oblivious to her change as she stopped and scanned the crowd, attracted to the movement of those around her. She relied on her senses as Devlin became an afterthought.

She glared under her brows at one young man jumping close by. Her instincts took over. With every fiber of her being, she desired his blood. When he left the dance floor, she trailed close behind, always vigilant for an opportunity to advance upon him. He approached the congested bar. Several objects crossed between her and her prey and with the strength she concealed before, she pushed all obstacles from her path.

The young man motioned for the bartender as she stood behind him, hearing not the music but the sound of his pulse in his jugular. She licked her lips, and all reservations about killing a man were gone. She tapped his shoulder and when the young man turned, she kissed him, cutting his lip with her fang. With the small trickle of blood she tasted, her eyes rolled back in her head in euphoria.

"Ouch," the young man said, then a tall woman pushed him aside to stand before Rebecca.

"Hey, what do you think you're doing?" yelled the woman. "This is my boyfriend, you skank."

The young woman swung at Rebecca but Rebecca moved faster and ducked. Another flip of her stomach awoke Rebecca's self-control. By the grimacing appearance of the young woman's face and the boy holding his lip, Rebecca grasped the potential danger of the situation. Backing away, she bumped into several people, until something grabbed her shoulder. She spun, claws drawn, prepared for an attack when she recognized Devlin's face.

"Why did you leave the dance floor?" Devlin asked. "What's wrong?"

There was no pulse in her chest. This scared her more than her desire to feed.

I feel weak and confused. What am I doing? I'm hungry? What time is it?

She checked her watch and kept her head low.

So hungry I can't even think straight. The blood bank! But it's clear across the park. And it's closed already. What am I going to do now, break in? Devlin can't find out, not yet. I'm not ready to tell him. But I can't stay here.

"I need to go," Rebecca yelled over the music.

"What? But we just got here," Devlin said. "Come on, we'll find a quiet place…"

"No, I feel ill," she said as she covered her mouth with her hand, self-conscious of her fangs.

Devlin nodded, grabbed her hand, and rushed her out beside him. Bodies everywhere, they passed some lining the hallways making out. Rebecca put her head down and pushed Devlin from behind until they reached the exit. He hit the door's release bar, and she shot past him. The moist, cool air filled her lungs but didn't extinguish the hunger.

"Stay here," she said as she headed for the street. "I don't want you to see me sick."

"Wait, Rebecca."

In the time they were in the night club, a thick fog crawled along the ground obscuring curbs and pot holes. Visibility reduced to only a few yards. Dodging pedestrians, cars and rickshaws, Rebecca reached the curb on the opposite side of the street. A quick glance back and Devlin stood with a puzzled gaze.

The fog thickened more as she entered the gate of Central Park. Flipping off her shoes, she ran with all her might. Trees, people, bridges, benches became a blur as she raced past. She felt free as the wind tossed her hair, but the hunger returned stronger than before.

The pounding in her head drowned out the world until she reached a deserted, dark part of the park. She ran until she approached a streetlight over a bench where five different cement paths met. She became aware of her surroundings, remained in the shadows as she listened to four separate heart beats close by. She smelled great fear.

Three men leaned over something Rebecca couldn't see at first. She heard a rip of what sounded like cloth and a shriek. A female whimper and pleaded with the men. She perceived a woman who lay in the grass. She resisted the one who centered himself between her legs while another held her arms down.

Two pedestrians approached, slowed, until one of the men looked up at them and pulled a switch blade. "Yeah, that's right, keep walkin." The couple put their heads down and rushed away.

"Please," the woman said. "Let me go."

She received a hearty laugh as the men pulled at her clothes and the one holding the knife kissed at her face. The woman screamed and kicked her legs which brought a slap from the man who leaned over her. Rebecca could smell the blood from the woman's busted lip. She salivated more. Fog concealed her well as she contemplated their fate.

A guiltless crime, or vigilante. Or am I just justifying my own selfish deeds? What would the honorable Lord Devlin do?

That wasn't hard for her to figure out. And a devious smile

grew.

From the shadows she walked under the streetlight. Placing her leg on the park bench, she adjusted her garter belt and extended the slit in her skirt to reveal more of her stockings and the clip that held it.

"Hey," Rebecca called as she left the bench and walked straight for the men.

One of the guys tapped the shoulder of another after he looked up. Rebecca knew she drew men like flies to honey and stopped at the edge of the light on the pavement. She shook her long hair, positioned her lips in a pouty way, and glared at them from under her brows.

"Move on, lady," the one with the switch blade said. He hovered over the woman as she cried softly. But the other two were snared by Rebecca's bait.

"Really?" Rebecca replied. "You'd want that scrawny thing over—me?"

The two broke off from their victim, each taking a position on either side of Rebecca. She encouraged their closeness, placing each of her hands on their chest to feel their hearts racing. They were young men not much taller than her. Punks or gang members, Carmichael would call them, with too much pride and too little sense. No matter, she saw them as food.

The predators are now prey.

The woman on the grass whimpered, which sent a shaft of hatred through Rebecca's heart as her fingernails and fangs tingled, growing longer.

Not even Devlin's kind preys on women. They will pay.

"I heard a song," Rebecca said. "Something like—it takes two to make it right, three makes it out of sight."

Rebecca tossed her hair revealing her perfect smile, flawless skin and inviting eyes. It happened whenever she left the safety of the manor. This time she used it for her own purposes. She stroked one of the men's cheeks and down his neck, resting her fingers gently along his jugular.

"What do you think four would be?" she asked with a devious smile.

The one holding the young woman pushed her away, rose to join his friends.

"*Run,*" Rebecca snarled at the woman.

The young woman scrambled to her feet, ran down the path, and disappeared into the fog bank. Rebecca motioned for the three men to follow her into a darker area on the cement path and out from under the bright streetlight. Anticipating her prey excited her more, almost to the point of sexual arousal. And they followed as sheep led to the slaughter.

"You'll regret this, lady," one of the men who drew near said. "You should have walked on."

Rebecca couldn't contain her smile as they circled her. She picked the one with the switchblade as her first victim and placed her cheek next to his. Her hands grazed the front of his pants as the others watched and made comments.

"You think your strong, don't you?" she whispered.

Her fingers coiled around his neck and under his jaw, lifting him so high that his feet dangled. Her other hand grabbed the man's hand that held the switchblade. Snapping his wrist, she pulled his arm close and pierced his arm with her fangs. The man let out a cry but only for a second, then collapsed to her feet unconscious as she tossed the knife away.

Eva was good practice in dosing a victim with venom to produce the desired amount of unconscious time. A thimble full rendered Eva out for more than a half-hour.

"Holy shit," another said.

The next one stood close enough for Rebecca to grab him by the greasy black hair. A bite on the side of the neck, and he fell as the first. She stepped over him and headed for the last one.

"You're a vampire?" he muttered tripping over a curb while searching his body for a weapon. "That's impossible."

He turned to run but Rebecca ran faster and met him at the edge of the lighted area.

"Ssssshhhh," she said. "Everyone will want to be one."

She grabbed his arm and spun him into her as if she danced the tango, but this time she led him. With his back to her, she plunged her fangs into his neck and he fell to her feet. Still holding his arm, she dragged him back to the others.

Chapter 26

Discovered

The low-lying ground mist enveloped Rebecca's victims. She knelt by the one, reentering the pierced site on his neck and sucked in the sweet nectar she longed for. The weeks of rationing melted away and her mind sharpened. With every suckle, she derived the benefit.

Only half done with her first course, she heard foot falls and her eyes rose to see Devlin at the edge of the path. Their eyes met, and she realized she couldn't hide any longer. Panic washed over her. Leaping to her feet, she turned to run down the path.

"*Stop!*" Devlin's voice erupted like a thunderclap and it startled her. She froze. "You know you can't outrun me."

"I can try," she said. "I'm not what I was."

Rebecca turned slowly as she heard his steps approaching. On the other side of the dark shadow Devlin paused as the fog conveniently covered the men laying beneath it. Yet, she experienced several odd emotions. Guilty for wanting to hide her score from him, selfish in wanting it all for herself, and pride for her kills. Then she filled with fear.

No unsanctioned.

And she couldn't hide her fear from him.

"I smell you, my little one," his voice unthreatening, soft and velvety again. "You have no cause to fear me."

"Yes, I do." She cautiously waited.

His expression changed to confusion. He shook his head and advanced, then stopped abruptly. "Is that blood on you? What happened? Are you alright? Are you bleeding?"

"Sssstay way." Her fangs felt obtrusive compared to her normal teeth.

"I can help you," he said. Devlin moved forward again but his foot snagged on something. He glanced down then back at Rebecca. "Is this—a person?"

Rebecca sensed he decerned the situation and her adrenaline provoked her predatory side of her again. "*Mine,*" she snarled, hissed and showed her fangs.

"Rebecca? How?" Devlin asked while edging closer. "Did you do this? Answer me."

Rebecca looked from Devlin to the men and covered her mouth, but her hands dripped with blood. Her eyes clouded with tears.

"I never wanted thiz," Rebecca muttered. "I'm thorry, I didn't know how to tell you."

"What's wrong with your mouth?" Rebecca smiled revealing her pink teeth and fangs. "Who turned you?"

"You did. When you zuckled on me to zave me from the gunthot wound."

"That was—so long ago," he muttered. "That's impossible. None of us in the family could do this except Olga."

Devlin stared at the victims then ran his fingers through his hair with a half-horror, half-epiphany expression. "Oh. God, I did, didn't I? You lost the inhibitor when the doctor removed your ovaries. They would've produced the estrogen I thought would keep you from turning. How stupid was I? I could have killed you."

Will he try to kill me now?

"Why didn't you tell me this when we met again?" Devlin asked.

"I only found out a few weekz ago," she said. "When Eva told me she had been adding blood to my food sssince—well a very long time."

"When did you feed last?"

"Yesterday, when I returned from the caterer," she replied. "But it waz only a few zipz off the blood bag."

"No, I mean, really fed?"

"You mean like thiz?" Rebecca pointed to the ground. "Maybe zirty dayz, no longer. The day of the carjacking."

"Why did you lie to me?"

"I didn't know how to tell you or explain what happened. Thiz iz all very new to me. I waz afraid of what you'd zink of me and turn on me. You wanted me like I waz. But I can't be that now."

"I won't turn on you," Devlin said. "Tell me everything."

"One of the carjackerz—touched me inappropriately. I waz afraid, then—angry, and that'z when everything changed. With

Eva's decline, she hadn't been spiking my food. I tried to manage on my own. But with all the changez in the house and you getting married, I was angry—emotional on top of hungry and tired. I snapped. I couldn't ztop myself. *I* fed on the first one, then cauzed the car to crash when I went after the driver."

"You were in the car when it crashed?"

She nodded.

"That was the last time?" he demanded. "And that was also the first time you truly fed?"

She noticed his anxiety. "Why?"

"How many blood packs do you consume in a day?" he asked.

"One bag lasted a few days before the accident," Rebecca said. She felt the hopelessness of the situation again. Her shoulders slumped. "I'm having trouble keeping to a bag a day now. They're expensive. They don't taste good. And I'm not sure I can obtain more. But everyday it's getting harder to maintain the rationing."

Devlin paced around the men.

"Are you going to kill me?" Rebecca asked with his silence.

Devlin glared at her as if she had just grown horns. "No, why would you think that?"

"No unsanctioned vampires, Eva warned me. Your family won't allow me to exist."

"That's not altogether true," Devlin said. "You're with me now. We'll deal with that later. And you've been unsettled since 1928 until recently?"

"Yes," Rebecca replied. "Eva took it upon herself to satisfy my hunger, fearing what I would do to the others if I began to starve. When I didn't recover well after I returned to the manor, Eva suspected what had happened and called the other servants of your family. She asked only certain questions so as to not arouse suspicion. They told her about being unsettled."

"She knew all those years and didn't tell me?" Devlin said. "That you were unsettled? I thought you had an aversion to blood."

"I thought so, too. Apparently, I was hungry." Rebecca licked her lips as she surveyed her kills. "I remained that way for decades and would still be the same if it had not been for the carjacking. I couldn't stop myself." Rebecca smelled the blood, heard it pounding in her ears like a bass drum. She covered her ears, but that was no use. She growled in frustration.

"Now, if you'll excuse me," she said. "I haven't eaten fresh—in a long while. And I can't control thiz right now."

"It's adrenaline," Devlin said. "It's prey-drive. You're in hunter mode. It overcomes your inhibitions. In time, you'll learn to use it as a tool, my love. But I understand what's happening to you. To gain control, calm yourself. Take a deep breath and exhale slowly. You don't want to maul the bodies. You see, this is why we maintain a feeding schedule. Cravings can make one— unpredictable."

Rebecca did as he said then turned back to one of the victims closest to her. She kicked him with enough force to flip him onto his back. Slightly conscious, instinctively the man raised his arms to shield his face as she hovered over him. Grabbing his elbow and fist, she sunk her teeth into his wrist. Bones snapped and blood flew. The man screamed.

Devlin waited, motionless as she finished feeding on the man. Then he moved within her line of sight and she hissed again.

"I understand, Rebecca." Devlin knelt to her level and leaned over one of the men. She scrambled to encounter him, fangs flaring. "These are your prizes. At your current level of thirst, you'll protect your kills. You did well and I don't want to take them from you."

Devlin leaned closer, and she impulsively snarled at him again.

"Sorry," she said. "I can't control anything."

"It's normal, love," Devlin said. "But smelling all this—is quite tempting. I doubt you'll consume them all. Would you consider sharing with me?"

Rebecca looked around at the bodies. The battle was a blur in her mind. But she realized what she had done. She nodded and pointed to the first attacked.

"Come," Devlin stood and held out his hand. "Come join me. This will be our first dinner together."

"You make it sound important." She took his hand, and he helped her up.

"It is," he replied. "Not all my wives made it through. I feared the change for you. You don't know how happy this makes me. Now there is nothing to hinder us from spend the rest of our lives together."

Once on her feet, Devlin took her in his arms, embracing her, then licked her from her chin to her temple.

"You taste fantastic," he said, beaming. "I love you."

Rebecca laughed, she missed his sense of humor, his boyish charm, his touch and his embrace. Reflecting on how easily she fell back into his arms, she wanted to love him again. They kissed only a little before even Devlin became preoccupied. Together, they walked to another victim. Her predator side relaxed.

As if he read her mind. "Don't think about it," he said, kneeling, grabbing the young man at the back of his head. "Here, I can teach you how to make the kills worthy of your effort." Devlin pointed with his long fingernails. "Femoral artery—largest in the lower extremities. But be careful. It splatters when punctured, especially if they're alert and filled with fear."

Devlin grabbed the upper torso, slamming him on his back again. Rebecca knelt beside him and ripped open the pants leg. Devlin traced the route of the artery along the upper thigh with his finger. She could hear the man's pulse increase, felt her tongue against her lips as she salivated, thinking of the red wine coursing through his veins. Rebecca slinked across the man's body as Devlin's hold kept the man from moving. Slowly he revived.

"Please don't," whispered the man, holding his broken arm with a bite wound.

Rebecca grinned thinking of the man's indiscretions, then nailed him in the leg with her fangs. Devlin punctured the man's neck. The man had no strength to fight them both. His body tensed and shook. Rebecca felt the lack of resistance and decreased heart rate, then glanced up at Devlin who appeared pleased.

"Why does it taste so much better?" Rebecca asked. She savored the flavor of this one above the others.

"Adrenaline, for one, gives it that wild flavor. It's why we eat live food and not dead. Second, blood type. You'll favor some over others just like you would chocolates or marinara sauces. And blood types matter, you won't like your own. Once we could analyze the difference between types, we discovered it."

"That's why you avoid…" she began.

"Yes, I don't care for blood that was once my own type."

Rebecca returned to her feast, but she knew she couldn't keep going.

"We don't have to torture them," Devlin said, then grinned. "But sometimes, I like to. You're so beautiful." He marveled as she fed. "Change of diet, how clever."

"I didn't lie."

"No, you didn't."

He smiled, each pink tooth outlined in crimson, then he returned to feasting. When finished, they both rested back on their knees. Rebecca's flesh felt energized.

"What now?" she asked. "We can't leave them here like this. The lack of blood will be—suspicious."

"Now, you're thinking like one of us." Devlin rose, his clothes spotted all over with blood, but not as bad as hers. "One body could fit in the trunk of the Rolls, but the Range Rover doesn't even have a trunk. What we really need is a ..."

"Van." Rebecca's tongue slipped over her fangs. "From the funeral, they're rented till tomorrow."

"Excellent." He pulled a cell phone out of his pocket. "Carmichael, sorry to wake you, old boy. Oh, you're awake. Yes, she's right here."

Devlin paused, and Rebecca heard Carmichael talking very loudly. At that moment she saw blood on her hands, under her nails, on her sleeves, and down her blouse. She wanted to wipe her mouth, but there was no place on her clothes that didn't have something spattered or soaked. Devlin, intuitively, handed her his handkerchief.

"Shut up and go to the house. Switch out the Range Rover for one of the vans. Take out a couple of the seats in the back and bring the eight-mil poly with you." Devlin paused as if listening. "Three, and we're near the center of the park. We'll meet you on the Hudson side. Call me when you arrive." He paused. "She's fine, more than fine. She's going to be my wife."

Devlin put his phone away and glowed. Watched the shadows around him for movement.

"You and Carmichael have done zisss before?" she asked, continuing with her slurred speech.

"It happens," he said with a snicker. "But it's been a long time, love. Now I know why he's acting like this."

"Why," Rebecca asked. "All the servants are acting odd."

"They want to become your Familiars. They want to serve you. When a new vampire is created, Familiars come out of the woodwork. Not in the same degree as once the change is complete. But it explains why you had such a hard time going out in public. The Familiars don't understand why they act the way they do. It's an unconscious thing. Like the man who insisted on dancing with you or that biker. All they know is that they want you."

"I hope ssso," Rebecca said. "It wazzz making me zink the world waz going crazzzy."

"I can't wait to teach you all I know. We don't have to hunt with the readily available inmates so close to home. But back in the day, I made this an art form."

"I don't zink I'm ready for that yet," she said.

Devlin walked to her first body. He knelt and checked him for a pulse, then tapped at the underside of his wrist.

"And these leftovers will go over well at home," he said.

"You make it sssound like Chinessse takeout. How are we going to get zem to the van?"

"We carry them. Did you see anyone when you attacked them?"

"Zey were going to rape zisss poor, defencelesss girl. But I offered them a willing victim and zey let her go. Ssshe ran when I told her to."

"She'll have called the police. And it may take them a while to find this place in the fog, but we need to move them now."

"But they're grown men? They must weigh between one-ssseventy-five and two- twenty each."

"You'd be surprised how strong you are now that you've

satisfied your hunger."

Chapter 27

Confessions

Five fifty-eight, just before dawn, the sun's light slowly crept over the trees and surrounding buildings. Central Park was desolate in the early morning hours. Devlin and Rebecca hid in the bushes near the gate where he had instructed Carmichael to meet them.

"When will zessse zingsss retract?" Rebecca asked with a slur as she touched her elongated canines. "Zey retracted fassster when I fed the firssst time."

Devlin let out a loud laugh.

"Zisss isssn't funny," she replied. "Ssstop laughing."

"And you ran from the scene of the accident. Adrenaline has a large effect on how our bodies work." He forced a straight face. "In the beginning, it can take a while, be patient." He suppressed a smirk as he looked away. "You sound like Sylvester the cat from those old cartoons."

"There they go." Her tongue ran over her teeth as they shrank.

Devlin covered his mouth with his blood, spotted hand, trying desperately to hold his laughter back. She waved an accusing finger at him standing over the body she had carried.

"Stop it," she snarled.

"Don't get angry." He waved a finger right back with a huge smirk. "They'll come out again."

Rebecca spotted the van as it stopped outside the park even before Devlin's phone rang. "He's here."

Carmichael backed up, jumping the curb to angle the rear-end of the van between the vertical wrought-iron uprights of the Central Park gate. He disembarked from the driver's seat and surveyed the surroundings nervously before opening the rear doors.

Devlin and Rebecca emerged from the shadowy under-growth each with the bodies they carried. As they approached, Carmichael carried a shiny, black roll of plastic from the van. He held one end as he tossed the rolled end onto the cement to unfurl it, then unfolded it for a widespread. Devlin dropped one corpse onto the plastic as Carmichael leapt over the unfurled roll to help him, but Devlin waved him off.

"I'm fine, help Rebecca," Devlin told Carmichael with an edge of annoyance in his voice.

Carmichael turned, jaw dropped, when Rebecca dropped a body off her shoulder. He grabbed the dead man's feet as Rebecca repositioned herself by the bodies head to carry it by the arms.

"Over this way," Carmichael said. "Are you alright? You're not hurt?"

"I'm fine," Rebecca said. "The blood isn't mine."

"We have another roll, if that one isn't enough," Carmichael said to Devlin as Devlin worked on the first body he laid on the plastic. "These are on the small side. I'm surprised you didn't catch and release." Then he chuckled.

"Wasn't my decision," Devlin muttered and glanced at Rebecca. Their eyes met as the corners of his mouth rose in a proud toothy grin. "But Hispanics are usually worth the fight because their blood runs hot."

Rebecca caught Carmichael's confused expression as he glanced between them. After Carmichael laid his part of the body on the plastic sheet, he knelt opposite her and they commenced to roll it. Devlin handled the first wrapped man, tossing him into the van like a sack of clothes. Rebecca and Carmichael finished the second. Devlin grabbed it out of the way as Rebecca and Carmichael spread another sheet of plastic and quickly moved the last body in place.

"Wait, she's like you?" Carmichael gasped.

"Yes," Rebecca replied with a smirk. "And I have been for a while now."

"Hurry up," Devlin said. "I can sense activity in the streets."

"I don't understand. How?" Carmichael asked. "If she—why can't I? Why didn't you tell me, Becca? Were you like this when we…"

"Don't go there," Rebecca said, knowing he was foolish for broaching the subject in front of Devlin.

Rebecca heard the bones in Devlin's hands pop as his fists clenched tight and a low grimace. With one hand Devlin grabbed the back of Carmichael's flannel shirt and tossed him several feet on the walk. A flash of speed, and Devlin towered over him again, lifted him, then dragged him around the side of the van. Rebecca saw the despised look Devlin gave Carmichael as he launched him against the side of the van, rocking it.

"It's a rental," Rebecca said hurrying to finish the last body. "I have to pay extra for dents."

Devlin pinned Carmichael against the side, jamming his elbow and forearm under Carmichael's chin. Pressing his throat, Devlin lifted him off his feet. Rebecca tossed the last body in the back and rounded the corner to see Carmichael's hands holding onto Devlin's arm as it held him up. Blood trickled past Carmichael's temple from a gash in his hair line.

"Because you would serve no purpose," Devlin growled. "You presume a place you shouldn't. You're not my friend, but my servant. You're a Familiar, nothing more. A simple call of nature."

Rebecca smelled Carmichael's fear and knew Devlin lied to him.

"Lord Devlin," Carmichael sputtered. "About my behavior— I don't know what came over me, but I've been loyal...."

"I know you were loyal," Devlin said. "And I know why you behaved as you did. You were simply bonding to another Vampire. But that is not the reason I'm angry." Devlin lowered Carmichael to be nose to nose with him. "I know you have history with her, but I'm back now." Devlin snarled showing full fangs. "But you touch her or come between Rebecca and I again, and I'll end you."

Carmichael stiffened and struggled to speak. "Understood."

Devlin released him and Carmichael slid to the ground on his hands and knees. He remained low as Devlin closed the back of the van. Rebecca stood over Carmichael and waited for him to rise. She could tell by the way he avoided looking at her that he was angry. She reached to help him but he snapped his arm from her touch.

"You shouldn't have said anything," Rebecca whispered.

"Carmichael," Devlin yelled from the other side. Carmichael rose and followed Rebecca around until they saw Devlin in the open side door.

"Did you bring the other things?" Devlin demanded.

Rebecca felt sorry for Carmichael. She didn't think he deserved it, considering Devlin's absence produced the opportunity for the tryst.

"Yes, sir," Carmichael said. "And something for the Mistress as well."

Devlin held his hand out to Rebecca. Receiving it, he helped her into the van.

"We don't have time to go to the new manor to exchange our clothes," Rebecca said.

"I know," Devlin replied. "That's why he brought these."

Carmichael produced two clear plastic-covered suits on hangers. Rebecca recognized it from her closet.

"I'm not sure I got everything you may need, Mistress," Carmichael said with down cast eyes. "Elizabeth helped me with the undergarments."

"Yes, yes," Devlin said abruptly. "What she doesn't have, we can buy. Now close the door so we can change."

"Here?" she asked. The doors closed and Carmichael turned his back. The windows were tinted, but Rebecca looked out nervously.

"Yes, here," Devlin replied. "We can't go to the bank covered in blood. We look like two psychopathic killers. The crime scene has enough blood to cause an investigation and we don't need any eyewitnesses saying they saw two people walking from the park with blood all over them. New clothes will only get us passed a hotel's front desk. Then we can clean up better. And you still have blood in your hair. Is there any way to hide that?"

"How's this?" Rebecca pulled it back and up with a rubber band.

"It will do for now," Devlin said.

Once dressed they exited out the side door again. Carmichael disappeared and Devlin hit the back of the van with his hand. The van lurched forward, then pulled out into the street.

"Shouldn't we go with him?" Rebecca asked as Devlin took her hand and they walked along the path back into the park.

"He'll head straight home to put what's left on ice. Ten a.m. will be here before you know it, and we need to shower and rest. Come on." They walked with the rising sun to their left. "I love this town. I've missed *the city that never sleeps.*"

"I didn't think you liked it that much. You don't spent long here and I never saw you go out at night or entertain."

"No. I'm a homebody for the most part, but on occasion, I

liked to roam the streets, alone."

"You lied again," Rebecca said. "To him, why?"

"Yes, to Carmichael, not to you. How do you know I lied to him?"

"I just do." Rebecca stopped. "What is the truth?"

"He shows the tendencies like those who fed freely, those my family opposed. He's always the first to place his cup to the hose. And he takes more than the others. I've given him special privileges because of his hunting abilities and assistance with body disposal. When I hunt, he's good at cleaning up the mess. He's jealous and wants to be like me. And after having you…"

"Nothing happened. I never slept with Carmichael."

"You didn't?"

She shook her head. Devlin looked relieved, taking her face in his hands, he kissed her passionately for a moment. But soon the park grew active with life. Devlin guided Rebecca through the park, emerged on the south side, then led her to the hotel on Central Park South. At the counter, he asked for a room, and slid a credit card to the woman behind the reception desk. Rebecca grabbed Devlin's hand, pulling it back from the counter noticing the dried blood framing his nail beds before he did.

"Thank you," Devlin whispered and gave her a kiss on the side of her face.

"You're welcome, darling," she replied.

Devlin's smile enlarged instantly.

"Lord Devlin," the woman said. "What size of room were

you looking for? The suite you normally occupy is taken until this evening."

"Just a room will be fine," he replied.

"Yes, sir." The woman returned to her typing. "Fourth floor will be alright?"

"Yes," Devlin replied.

When the woman handed the key card in the neat folder, Rebecca grabbed it quickly, nodded and smiled. Rebecca hoped the woman didn't notice her hands either. Devlin led her to the elevators, not letting anything or anyone between them, then waited. When the doors opened, many people rushed out and Devlin pulled her out of the way.

Once emptied, Devlin gestured for her to enter, then right behind her, punched the fourth-floor button. As the doors closed, Devlin waited under the floor-indicator lights. But after, as fast as lightning, he pinned Rebecca to the side wall. His body pressed hers as his lips found her lips and their tongues clashed. His one hand found her breast, then slid and grabbed her thigh as she lifted it and wrapped it around him. Rebecca absorbed him and responded with her own passion. Gently running her hand from his shirt, down past his waist, feeling the growing lump below his belt.

When the doors opened on the fourth floor, Devlin stood under the numbers again, glancing up, and Rebecca couldn't repress the devious grin. They held each other's hands and pressed close as they walked calmly and passed a couple who boarded the lift after them.

"Good morning," Devlin said.

"Good morning," the man replied as his eyes scanned Rebecca.

She felt Devlin's hand tighten around hers and knew the jealousy he felt.

"Don't worry," she whispered. "I'm all yours."

Rebecca had to let go of his hand to open the door, but Devlin didn't let go of her. He hovered behind her, and she felt his arousal press against her ass. His hands slid around her ribs. She opened it and they both slipped in, departing the outside world with the closing of the door. Before she could replace the keycard in the folder, Devlin's lips found hers and they kissed lingering longer than before.

It was as if last night never happened. How I wished some of it hadn't. Wait a tick, am I engaged?

Rebecca stripped off her blouse, as Devlin took off his shirt. They tossed their clothes onto a chair. The sight of him reminded her of the times they spent in each other's arms. It was almost too tempting to take advantage of him at that moment. She pulled him close as Devlin grabbed her around the middle. He touched her face and kissed her forehead. But she didn't want him to stop. Her hunger abated, she looked to other desires long unfulfilled. But he pulled away.

"Right now, we both need to shower and prepare for our obligations," Devlin said. "Like the bank."

"How can you think about *money* after last night?" she asked. She grabbed the rim of his pants and belt, pulling him against her.

I like being strong enough to manhandle him. This does have its advantages.

"How can you think of *that* after last night?" he asked with a grin.

The thought of the men she killed sobered her, feeling as if she should be more remorseful.

"You're right," Rebecca said and stepped back.

"Normally, I would encourage you, love," Devlin said as he led her to the bathroom. "But we need to wash off the evidence. And rest before we go out into public again. Just a kip, or we may not sleep at all, but we do need rest. Ladies first."

The hot water poured through her hair, over her shoulders and down her body. A red swirl pooled at her feet before disappearing down the drain. It felt good, erasing the event as it removed the blood from her hair and skin. Devlin waited with her towel and wrapped her in it the moment she stepped out, lovingly caressing her body.

"Now," she playfully scolded. "It's your turn."

Chapter 28

Regret

Rebecca sat at the small table wrapped in a white towel while Devlin showered. She felt the weight of the men's death and wanted to cry. Burying her head in her arms, she wept until she felt a warm hand on her bare shoulder. Devlin sat across from her with only a towel around his waist as she sat up.

"I know you never wanted this." Devlin reached across the table and took her hands in his. "But I'm not sorry."

"Did you intentionally change me?"

"*No*," he said. "I'd never do that without your consent. It was an accident, I swear. When we choose a bride, and the family gives their approval, Aunt Olga usually turns them. I've never turned one of my brides."

"Why her?"

"Through the decades, she's had a better success rate than us men. We get—anxious and usually kill our brides by trying to speed up the process. It takes months for a woman's body to accept the venom. She's learned to introduce their bodies to it slowly. Even then, it doesn't always take. I've had to kill some women who refused once they found out what I am, but more have died in the changing."

"This isn't reversable, is it? Like in the movies, by killing the head vampire?"

"I'm sorry, no," Devlin said with a smirk.

"It's not funny," Rebecca replied as her shoulders slumped and she sighed.

"This isn't lore, or magic, or some fantasy—it's science."

"Will you die if you go into the sunlight? No, of course not, I've seen you in daylight. Does sunlight do anything to you?"

"Like everyone else with an Anglo/Saxon Geno—burn like a lobster."

"Garlic?" Rebecca stood, then paced in front of him.

"Breath mints? But no adverse effects. But seriously, who wouldn't want to avoid bad breath? And I know what you're thinking, yes, a stake through the heart will kill me, just like everyone else. I just might not stay dead long. Any other lore you need to be straightened out?"

"Blood?" Rebecca said. "Am I restricted to only human blood?"

"For your sake, I wish I could say no. I'm sorry. Nothing will sustain you like human blood."

"How can you do this?"

"I was brought up by vampires, so for me to change into one was like a rite of passage. It felt normal for me. I can't imagine what you feel."

"If I was unsettled when I saw you feed in the dungeon. Why did I react so badly?"

"My theory is he had the same blood type as you," Devlin said. "It tastes stale."

"Eva gave me tomato juice once that tasted awful," Rebecca replied. "I've never tasted it like that since."

"Eva had clear instructions to stay away from my old blood type." Devlin stood. "She was a clever woman, she probably made the connection and avoided that type, whatever it was."

Rebecca leaned her head on his shoulder. His embrace soothed her fears.

"You said it's science, how?" she asked.

"It's a virus."

"If it's a virus, then a cure can be developed."

"No, unlike normal viruses, you can't develop an immunity. This virus affects the very molecules you're made of. As you know, it's not an airborne virus. It's saliva and blood. We've only found this out in the past fifty years. There's no going back once infected."

"Then how is it all the servants aren't changed?" she asked.

"It takes a bite," Devlin said. "Not a nibble or a suckle. And venom without blood isn't enough. It takes both in a quantity more than I give anyone. We've made mistakes, like feeding and not ensuring the victim is dead, but mostly with men. They are easier to turn, more accepting of the venom. For a woman, estrogen is an inhibitor. It's why I kept giving you venom after you healed from the wound and during your fevers. I figured you'd heal before the change happened. I can't believe I almost killed you trying to save you."

Rebecca took his face in her hands. "But you didn't. You saved me."

Devlin looked deeply into her eyes and struggled a smile.

"But know this," she said. "Since you saved me, my life has not been what I wanted. There have been times I wished you and Eva had let me die. If you leave me again, I'll look for a way out of this. I won't be *one of you*, if I can't be with you."

"I understand," he said. "I'm not leaving you again."

Devlin caressed her cheek as his eyes met hers. "You have been both my strength and my weakness. I want you on whatever terms you make. I'm more your slave now than you have ever been my servant. I can't live without you. I don't know how I could anymore."

Rebecca pressed her lips to his as their tongues met. She felt his arms tighten as their bodies contoured to each other. The passion they shared surpassed anything she had known with him before. They kissed and fondled until Devlin pulled away again. He resisted her advances.

"Not till you say you'll marry me," he said.

He must be joking.

She reached for him, but he held her off.

"I thought we settled this before we went to the nightclub?" Rebecca asked.

"No, you didn't say yes to my proposal," Devlin said.

"I heard you demanding, but not a proposal. Maybe you didn't pose the question the way a woman needs to hear it. You know I am old-fashioned."

Devlin dropped to his knees in front of her. Looking up from below in only a small white towel. Irresistible with his wet hair messed and not a blemish on his skin. But those dark eyes caught hers and she froze. He took each of her hands in his, kissed them, then took a deep breath.

Is he nervous? Surely, he's done this enough that it should be easy.

"Will you marry me, Rebecca Bellows?" Devlin asked, sincerely.

She nodded. "Yes, I'll marry you."

Devlin smiled up at her and kissed her hands again. He held up one finger, stretched past her for his pants and withdrew something from the pocket. Just a flash told her it was something gold. Back on his knees in front of her, he placed a ring on her finger.

"It was my mother's," Devlin said.

"It's beautiful." She held the three carats as it reflected the light. It was the largest rock she had ever seen.

"I vowed no woman would ever wear her ring again unless they made me feel as valued and loved as she did. Only two others wore this ring. I hope you don't mind."

"What happened to them?" Rebecca asked.

"Jesra never made it through her change, and Ester died

during one of London's many plagues. They called it the Sweats. She died within twenty-four hours. We had been together only a few months."

"I'm sorry you had to go through that," she said touching his face.

He leapt into her arms and as they kissed, the towel fell from around her. Kissing more led to more intimate fondling. Devlin dropped his towel and her expectation rose as nothing separated them. Tumbling together onto the bed, she pulled him on top of her as her legs slid up his thighs. Devlin wrapped his arms around her, giving in to her advances. Her senses heightened, feeling him enter her; the sensations of his thrusts drew her quickly to her end. Devlin smiled down as she groaned, and her orgasm erupted within her. It was like the satisfied ending to a long, dramatic play that had been filled with both laughter and tears. Devlin followed soon after, indicated by his moans and final thrusts. He crumbled to her side, pulling her to him. Lovemaking in her new state fulfilled her more than ever before. Angled tightly, skin against skin, they fell asleep in each other's arms.

Chapter 29

End of Bellows

Devlin caressed her arm as she lay against his chest and didn't want to move. His occasional breath and heartbeat no longer bothered her. She cherished every moment of their intimacy.

"I fell asleep," Rebecca said groggily. "I thought we don't sleep after we're changed?"

"Sex has that effect on us." Devlin held her tighter. "It's the only sleep we're allowed. The only dreams we have are after sex. It's one of the reasons we desire a mate. Eternity is a wasteland without love."

"Did you dream?" she asked.

"Always." He touched her face and kissed her neck. "I always dream of you. Which really made it quite hard to start over with anyone else. Thank you for that." His sarcasm made her smile.

"I'm not sorry." She tightened her hold on him. "You should have been with me these last four years."

"No, that isn't what I meant." Devlin held her face as he looked deeply into her eyes. "I've dreamt about you since you came into my life. After every woman I had, I had a Rebecca-chaser that haunted me. I thought I was going mad. I couldn't drown you out of my head with liquor or forget you in the arms of another. I should have known, if you haunted me like that, that you were still alive. But I had no way of knowing."

"That I am sorry for," she said. "And for that, I will make it up to you forever."

Devlin glowed.

"What do we do now?" she asked.

"We finish the business we have in the city and go home."

"Home," she echoed. "That sounds nice."

"You know, for all intents and purposes, you *are* already Lady Englewood. Due to the precariousness of changing a woman, the moment you became unsettled we were literally married. A wedding is just a formality."

"A wedding is not a formality," Rebecca said. "A wedding ceremony marks the passing from being alone to belonging." She bit her lip and insecurity took hold. "How many have you had?"

"Let me think," Devlin said. His eyes rolled and a smirk appeared on his lips. "Maybe ten."

"Ten?" she gasped. "I guess you wouldn't want another ceremony. I don't want to make you do something you don't want to do."

Disappointed, Rebecca sat up and moved to the edge of the bed.

"Oh, no." Devlin grabbed her, tossing her back down, and began to tickle her. "Don't say that. I've seen and heard that before.

Every time a woman says that, I live to regret it. If you want a wedding, I don't care about the size or expense. You shall have it. But I'm too busy to help you plan it."

"I don't know if I want one. I mean, who would I invite? My families gone and I don't have friends outside the house."

"Just the staff, my family, and my business associates. If it's important to you, then it's important to me. And it would mark my retirement from public life. If I just disappear, everyone wonders where I went. I've even faked my own death. But if I marry, they figure I'm domesticated and starting a family. I'll need a good forty to sixty years before I can show my face again as Devlin Jr."

"We had better get ready for the bank," Rebecca said.

He followed her to the bathroom as she showered again. He shaved, fighting with the foggy mirror. He swiped it with his hand as she emerged and dried off.

"No privacy?" she asked, sarcastically.

"No, never again, my love," he said with a grin. "I'm not letting you out of my sight. And what a sight."

Devlin lifted his chin, but his eyes followed her.

"Come to think of it," he said. "After the bank, we'll need to do some shopping."

"For what?"

"New clothes."

"But you have a ton of suits at the house. You're such a metrosexual," she said and smacked his naked ass.

"I am not," Devlin said. "I like women."

"Not homosexual, metrosexual," she said. "Look it up."

"The clothes are for you," he replied. "You're a lady now, and the thrift store look won't do. You need to look elegant, stylish, and smart for when you enter the manor *and* for when you meet my family. You'll fill a tangible place in my life, and you need to rise to that level. Clothes symbolize that change. And for my family to take you seriously, you need to look the part. Negative first impressions can be hard to overcome. Usually, Olga goes over all this while she's changing a woman."

"I refuse to look like a mindless fashion model."

"You don't have to. But quality is important. My aunts know quality when they see it."

"Your family?" she said. "Don't terrify me so soon. What if they don't like me?"

"Non-sense, they'll love you."

"You're lying again."

"How do you know if I am or not?"

"Woman's intuition."

"Where my family is concerned, I should speak to them alone before you meet them."

"Why?'

"Just to explain everything then we should throw a little party for them and to publicly announce our engagement. After a year, we'll get married. That should be enough time to plan, right?"

"How should I know. I've never planned a wedding. But we can get the clothes later. The staff knows me, I'm not impressing anyone at the house."

"That's the problem. They'll take you for granted as their Madam or Mistress," he said. "The servants respect the difference between our kind and them by clothing, status, and money, not just venom. The moment we arrive at the manor, the ties of you being a servant must be severed. Carmichael will arrange my normal meet and greet at which time we'll announce you as *my fiancé*."

"Are you going to explain everything?" she asked. "That I've been *like you* this whole time?"

"No, just that I've chosen you as my wife, and that you need to be treated as if you already are one of my kind. We'll have to work out the house manager between us, share the responsibilities until we choose a replacement. You said there were servants who should have the chance at your job."

"I wasn't serious. Most of them don't have it in them."

"That's the problem with Familiars. They're better followers than leaders. Madam Eva was great, because she wasn't a Familiar. She was like a wife and mother to me. I didn't need to be so involved here as I do in my other estates."

"Maybe I can stay on as the house manager. Just manage from afar."

"That never worked for me," Devlin said. "The household seems to fall apart when there isn't a manager lurking about."

After he finished his shave, he sat on the bed and picked up the room phone.

"Front desk? Yes, please reserve the bridal suite for this

week, if it's available."

"We're staying?" she asked.

"Yes," he said to her with a coy smile. Then, he addressed the desk helper again. "About six days. And my driver will need his usual spot. Black sedan, stretched slightly." Devlin held his hand over the mouthpiece. "They want to know the make and model."

Rebecca took the phone from his hand.

"2017 Range Rover HSE, and only an extra door length not a full stretch," she said to the desk clerk.

"It's been reserved," the man on the other end said. "Will that be all?"

"No, I'd like a bottle of scotch brought to the new room," she asked. "And that will be all. Thank you."

"Good, now call Carmichael and arrange for him to join us," Devlin said, disappearing into the bathroom. Rebecca picked up her cell and found his number when Devlin popped his head out. "And love…"

"Yes," she replied, glowing.

"I love you, Lady Englewood," Devlin said and disappeared again. "I love the way that sounds."

She heard the shower burst onto the tile floor, then he began to sing, but not well. She snickered to herself.

Life is only going to get more interesting from here on. But I can't wait.

"Carmichael," she paused. "It's—Lady Englewood."

The End

ABOUT THE AUTHOR

K. A. Monaco, born in Pennsylvania, now a resident of Maryland with her beloved husband, Mark, and their two frisky sibling English Setters. She holds a Bachelor of Science, but her first love is writing which began early in life. She belongs to many writer's support groups and has already produced many works to-be-published. A current theme through her books are strong confident woman characters who must face and overcome obstacles to live fulfilled lives. Romance is not her sole genre; enjoys science fiction, fantasy, and action/adventure as part of each book. And perhaps a bit of horror at times. She weaves obscure details all thru her writing from her personal interests in psychology, the erotic mind, other cultures, physics, faith, and language. She hopes that in reading her books, you may feel yourself peering into a mirror, for insight into yourself and human behavior in general.

Contact the author at:
kimberlyamonaco22@gmail.com